RIVER RAID

The Scorpion Squad Series
Book Four

Eric Helm

Also in the Scorpion Squad Series

Body Count

The Nhu Ky Sting

Chopper Command

RIVER RAID

Published by Sapere Books.

20 Windermere Drive, Leeds, England, LS17 7UZ,
United Kingdom

saperebooks.com

ISBN: 978-1-913335-35-9

This book is for J. Gomoll, who offered a special kind of friendship when I most needed it; for R. Russell, whom I tried to dislike, but couldn't; and for the Spike; for M. Roberts, who was a better friend than I knew; and for A. Hooper, because he played the Stones.

It's also for Carrie, who loved me once, and whose eyes were never blue.

But mostly for Shannon and the nurse, because I owe it to them.

A very special thanks to W. Bassett, R. Bunnell, J. Cornett, S. Guffey, W. Howe, H. Kepner, J. Lamb, and J. Swaby, who in their own way, helped to get the damned thing done.

AHN TAP

Ong Ngoc had been hanged by the neck from the big tree in the center of the market with a strand of barbed wire; he had been allowed to slowly strangle to death while he was emasculated. His hands were bound behind him with more wire.

Around the neck … had been hung a sign, warning the villagers not to cooperate with the Americans and their puppet soldiers from Saigon.

"The VC make a serious miscalculation," explained Truong Trinh. "We can no longer tolerate the VC among us. From this moment on, Ahn Tap no longer be a safe place for the Viet Cong."

Although the old chief did not know it, from that moment on, Ahn Tap would no longer be a safe place for anyone.

PROLOGUE

THE VILLAGE OF AHN TAP, RVN
NOVEMBER 1964

With great interest, Le Quan Kim watched the construction of the new school by the American soldiers with the funny hats and big noses. Truly it was a thing of great beauty, made of painted white boards with black-trimmed windows and doors. The windows even had glass! And inside there were blackboards to write on with big, new pieces of chalk, never used before, and four rows of six wooden desks, each with its own chair. At the front of the room there was a great oak desk and chair for the teacher, who would soon arrive from Saigon, and out front, on a wooden pole, a big brass bell to call the students to school.

Le was very happy that the teacher would come soon, for he wanted very much to learn to read and write. He had been taught how to write his name by Ong Ngoc Diem Bai, the elderly gentleman who owned one of Ahn Tap's two small general stores, but Le wanted to learn how to unlock the mystery of books himself.

Le knew about books. Ong Ngoc sometimes read stories to him about faraway lands peopled by sailors who went all the way around the world in their boats, or fought great battles on horseback with swords, or flew through the sky in rockets. Le did not really believe you could fly through the sky in a rocket, but he did like the story — almost as much as the one about the little girl who stepped through a mirror to drink tea with a hare.

Ahn Tap was a pleasant village on the northern bank of the Song Tien Giang, which many people called the Mekong River. Actually a collection of three tiny hamlets, Ahn Tap 1, 2, and 3, it had grown up around a Japanese army outpost during World War II. The locals, given to a diplomatic, philosophical bent of mind, had, in the interests of survival, little difficulty reaching an accommodation with the Japanese, or with the French Legionnaires who came after them. And while the villagers sometimes wondered why so many of the French Legionnaires spoke German, they found them much more likable than the Japanese, and under the Frenchmen who spoke German, the village grew modestly prosperous.

But still, there was no school. And out of a population of nearly 1,500, there were perhaps two dozen citizens who could read and write.

After the French had come the Viet Cong, who spoke of the evils of the French and their playboy puppet in Saigon, and their running dog American lackeys, and spoke of educating the people to the truth of democratic socialism. But while they sometimes lived with the villagers and took their food and slept with their daughters, they did not build a school.

And then came the big-noses with the funny hats. And they brought with them fierce Nùng-Tai tribesmen, whom the villagers feared but respected, and Saigon soldiers, whom the villagers neither feared nor respected. And they announced that they would build a school.

Most of the villagers seemed pleased that Ahn Tap would finally have a school. The village chief, Truong Trinh Vinh, made a long speech welcoming the Americans to Ahn Tap and thanking them for their generosity. It was the same speech he had made when the Viet Cong first came to the village, but the

Americans did not know that, and so they were pleased by the welcome.

But not everyone in the village was pleased to see the Americans come or to have them build a school. The Viet Cong who lived in the village said the school was merely a trick of the Americans and the Saigon government for creating false propaganda and subverting the loyalty of the villagers to the revolutionary struggle to reunify the country.

When the school was finished, the VC called a meeting of the villagers in the town square and spoke of the school as a symbol of evil. They also spoke of things like Marxist-Leninist socioeconomic theory of proletariat revolution, whatever that was, and warned that the Americans had come to bring war to the village and to burn the villagers' huts and rape their women. They said the Americans were dupes of the puppet leaders in Saigon, and that the Saigon government was the puppet lackey of the Americans. And that the new school was a symbol of the treachery of both.

One of the village elders, Ong Duong Ben Ban, questioned the VC political cadre leader about how the Americans could be dupes of the Saigon government and the Saigon government puppets of the Americans at the same time. He pointed out that it was the Viet Cong, not the Americans, who taxed the villagers, and that it was the Viet Cong, not the Americans, who slept with their women.

After he was done talking, the VC political cadre chief said that Ong Duong would be taken away to a re-education camp, where these apparent contradictions would be explained to him. His re-education must have taken a long time. That was the last the villagers ever saw of him.

Two nights later, some of the Viet Cong who lived in the village showed their contempt for the new school by burning it to the ground and throwing the bell into the river.

The next morning, most of the villagers said nothing, remembering the lesson of the elder who had been taken away to be re-educated. But Mr. Ngoc, the shopkeeper, was openly critical of the unknown arsonists. Times were changing, he said, and it was important for all the children of Ahn Tap to leam to read and write. To burn the school in the middle of the night, he said, was not the act of warriors, but of cowards. These were serious words and did not win Mr. Ngoc any friends among the VC party members and sympathizers in the village.

The village chief took a more moderate view. When the big-nose American Bac Si Washington came with Bac Si Tam to conduct their weekly health clinic, the chief told them that the burning of the school was an unfortunate incident. He explained that the villagers did not share the view of the VC that the school was a bad thing, but since the Americans and Saigon were at war with the VC, it was only natural that the VC would take offense at the Americans erecting a building in Ahn Tap and try to destroy it. He said he hoped the Americans understood this, and would take no reprisals against the villagers.

The American Bac Si listened politely to the village chief as Tam translated for him, then laughed and smiled.

"Sergeant Tam, tell him we understand," said Washington. "And that there will be no reprisals. Instead, tell him that we will build a new and better school to show our continuing support for educating the youth of Ahn Tap, and that the teacher will arrive in a few weeks as planned."

Bac Si Tam translated the message, and the village chief went away with a relieved expression on his face.

So the Americans rebuilt the school. They built it so that it would not burn. They built it out of concrete blocks and cement, with steel chairs and desks, and put up a new bell to replace the one thrown into the river.

When the school was finished, they painted it bright red.

Bac Si Washington told the chief in very serious tones that they had painted it such a bright color so that the VC would know that it was only a school, and not a military installation, and therefore would have no reason to destroy it.

A week later, the new schoolteacher, Co Bang Mai Thuot, was brought to the village by the Americans and introduced to the chief and the elders.

Co Bang was a very young woman, too young to be a teacher, thought several of the villagers. But she had a degree from the university in Saigon, was from a good family, and seemed particularly fond of children, so she was quickly accepted by the villagers. Miss Bang was also very pretty, which made her classes unusually popular with the older boys and young men of Ahn Tap, and there was much speculation over whether or not she might marry someone from the village. But while she had many suitors, she continued to live alone in the blue cement house that the Americans had built for her next door to the school.

Co Bang taught classes six days a week, from noon until four-thirty. She could not teach in the mornings before it became hot, because that was when the villagers worked the fields and paddies, and she could not teach in the late afternoon and evening because that was when the villagers fished the river. Co Bang understood this, and adapted her teaching schedule to the villagers, rather than trying to force them to conform to hers.

In her one-room school she taught basic mathematics, French, English, Vietnamese, and Vietnamese history. Despite some pressure from the district capital and Saigon, she did not at first teach politics, pointing out that there was little value in trying to explain abstract concepts like democracy to people who could not yet write their own names or perform basic arithmetic. Especially when the government advocating the teaching of democracy had come to power by a military coup, although this thought she kept to herself.

Le Quan Kim quickly became Co Bang's star pupil. The young orphan boy who lived in Ahn Tap 2 with his aunt and uncle was a natural student. He learned quickly, and seemed to almost have a hunger for knowledge. In spite of the necessity of helping his uncle with their four-acre farm and fish traps, Le quickly became the school's outstanding student.

One day, Co Bang questioned the boy about his study habits, and learned that Ong Ngoc had been helping him with his studies at night. This unusual effort on the part of the shopkeeper interested the teacher, and she had Le arrange an introduction for her. She fast became friends with the old gentleman, and through him became aware of the subtle, but pervasive influence of the Viet Cong in the village, later confirmed by her own observation of VC tax collectors.

It was only after Mr. Ngoc related the story of Mr. Duong, who had been taken away to be re-educated, that Co Bang began to include simple political lessons in her teaching. She did not know that one of her pupils was a Viet Cong spy.

In a village the size of Ahn Tap, few secrets were possible. It is difficult not to know what your neighbor is doing when you are living in his lap, and the expected birth of a new child was often announced by the cries of his conception. Thus, it was widely suspected that Truc Nguyen Bong was a VC agent. He was a known associate of VC sympathizers in Ahn Tap 3, and was overly careful in his avoidance of known VC sympathizers in Ahn Tap 2, the largest of the hamlets and the one in which he lived. Yet he was of the village and the villagers took care of their own. They did not betray him to the Americans or the Saigon soldiers, everyone was simply careful about what they said in his presence.

Everyone, that is, except Co Bang.

Miss Bang had not lived in the village long enough to understand village politics and know who to be careful around. Where Truc Nguyen Bong was concerned, Co Bang made two very serious mistakes. She openly discussed her political views in front of him in the classroom, and she rejected him as a suitor.

One Saturday morning, when the villagers got up early to prepare for the busy day of commerce ahead of them, they found an unusual sight awaiting them in the marketplace. Co Bang and Ong Ngoc had preceded them to the market sometime during the night and had remained there waiting for them.

Ong Ngoc had been hanged by the neck from the big tree in the center of the market with a strand of barbed wire; he had been allowed to slowly strangle to death while he was emasculated. His hands were bound behind him with more wire.

Co Bang had been similarly bound, and had Mr. Ngoc's severed manhood forced into her mouth. Her lips had then been sewn shut, and she had been impaled on a sharpened bamboo stake.

Around the neck of each victim had been hung a sign, warning the villagers not to cooperate with the Americans and their puppet soldiers from Saigon.

It was a sight calculated to sicken and terrify all the villagers. In this it was very effective. It was also an object lesson intended to frighten the villagers into cooperating with the Viet Cong and rejecting the Americans and South Vietnamese soldiers from the nearby Special Forces Camp. In this, it was much less effective.

When Bac Si Washington and Bac Si Tam arrived in Ahn Tap late that morning to hold their weekly clinic, the village chief told them what had happened to the new schoolteacher and her elderly friend, and showed them the bodies.

Then he told them that the Viet Cong had been using sampans to run supplies down the river at night from their sanctuaries in Cambodia, and that one such convoy was expected to pass the village that very night. Lastly, he gave them the names of everyone in the Ahn Taps whom he suspected of being Viet Cong.

"The VC make serious miscalculation," explained Truong Trinh. "They murder brutally a respected member of our community, and a young woman who chose of her own free will to become a part of our village. We can no longer tolerate the VC among us. From this moment on, Ahn Tap no longer be a safe place for the Viet Cong."

Although the old chief did not know it, from that moment on, Ahn Tap would no longer be a safe place for anyone.

CHAPTER 1

THE MEKONG RIVER REGION, REPUBLIC OF VIETNAM

First Lieutenant Jonathan Bromhead lay in the mud, and alternately watched the murky surface of the slowly flowing river in front of his M-14 bipod, and the muddy water gradually filling his foxhole.

Bromhead cursed softly to himself. He'd been a regular, if not necessarily devout, attendee of Mass back in his high school days in Kirksville, Missouri, and later at West Point, and in all that time he couldn't recall a single incident when he'd taken the Lord's name in vain. It was, he reflected, truly amazing how much his vocabulary had broadened since joining the U.S. Army Special Forces. He'd found a lot to swear about since then. The grueling, early morning runs at Ft. Benning and Ft. Bragg. The survival school in the Canal Zone. The simulated tactical exercise in the Everglades with the night jump where he'd broken a thumb and two toes. He'd learned to live with the pain after a week and a half in the Florida swamps eating turtle and alligator and water moccasin. Tonight he cursed the mud and the cold and the mosquitoes feasting upon the exposed flesh of his face and hands, and the lack of punctuality of the Viet Cong.

The Viet Cong had never been famous for their predictability, but Bromhead had held high hopes that tonight might be different. The VC frequently used the river network flowing into the IV Corps area of Vietnam to ship munitions from their sanctuaries just inside Cambodia to their forces fighting just inside South Vietnam, or as a source of revenue, holding up river traffic and taxing peasants on their way downstream to market with their cargoes of rice, fish, and woven mats and baskets. However, according to new intelligence reports, the Viet Cong had begun running supplies downriver on a regular schedule. This information was gathered on the frequent patrols conducted by the Special Forces men and their South Vietnamese and ethnic Tai allies, working out of the fortress-like camp they had established in the area earlier in the year. This information had been confirmed by the network of informants and agents established in the villages of the district by Sergeant First Class Derek Kepler, the Green Berets' intelligence specialist, and his LLDB counterpart, Trung Si Tran. The news that the Cong were now keeping to a regular timetable with their shipments of arms and ammunition had presented an opportunity too good to pass up.

Bromhead, the executive officer for the Special Forces A-Detachment at Camp A-555, had led a fourteen-man ambush patrol out through the perimeter defenses of the camp just after dark with the aim of convincing the VC that perhaps using the river to ship supplies was not such a hot idea after all. He had selected a spot for the ambush site about two klicks southeast of the camp, at a point where the Bassac River, although fairly wide, was shallow, and the current slow. Bromhead had deployed his men on the point of the sandbar that jutted well out into the river. Although it offered little in the way of natural cover, it reached almost a third of the way across the river, permitting the ambush party to bring a wide area of the channel and the far bank under effective small arms fire. The men reached the site shortly after nine-thirty, and dug in to wait for the VC.

And they had waited, and waited, while the mosquitoes and sandfleas gorged themselves on the men's blood, and the foxholes filled with water, and the night air turned chill, and one of the radios had gotten waterlogged and quit working. The backup radio was showing increasing signs of obstinance, and there was still no sign of the Viet Cong.

Bromhead had just about decided that the evening's activities were a bust, and he might as well call it a night and take the men back in for some hot food and dry clothes, when he heard the unmistakable thunk of wood on wood, and a few minutes later the dim outline of a single sampan came into view from upstream. The vessel was showing no lights, and staying well out in midchannel.

The absence of any lights or conversation aboard the boat, combined with the late hour chosen for its excursion down the river, left little doubt in Bromhead's mind that it was a Viet Cong sampan, but it was only a single vessel. Bromhead was after bigger game. The Intell reports had indicated that the VC were running miniconvoys of as many as six or seven sampans at a time. Bromhead hoped the sampan was a point scout for a larger group, and he let the boat pass by unchallenged. He passed the word quietly to his men to hold their fire, and silently hoped to hell he'd guessed right.

Bromhead's patience was rewarded five minutes later when the dim yellow light of a kerosene lantern shone several hundred yards downstream. The sampan had put into the far bank and lighted a lamp. There could be little doubt that it was intended as a signal, perhaps to indicate that the sampan had passed the sandbar without incident. Bromhead again passed the word among his men, telling them to unsafe their weapons and get ready, but cautioning them that no one was to fire until he did.

A few minutes later, three sampans came slowly around the bend in the river. Like the first, they were running without lights, and keeping well out in midchannel.

After the one radio had quit working, Bromhead had taken the second unit and placed it on the surface of the sandbar, next to his foxhole. That left the radio exposed to any incoming fire, but he figured it was better than giving it a bath in his foxhole. He now reached for the handset and attempted to call the camp and advise them that he had three enemy sampans in sight, and was preparing to engage them. His efforts were answered only by static. Evidently, the water had gotten to the second radio as well, despite his efforts to keep it dry. Disgusted, he tossed down the handset, and felt the ground next to the radio for one of the hand flares he had laid out earlier, identifying the one he wanted by its position closest to the radio.

As the sampans neared the point of the sandbar, Bromhead shouted to them in Vietnamese, telling them to come into shore, or they would be fired upon.

There was an excited chattering from the nearest of the boats, followed by silence; they continued on around the point of the sandbar. They obviously had no intention of stopping.

Bromhead sighed deeply. Well, he thought, I did my part. I gave them a chance to surrender.

He removed the protective end cap from the flare, which also contained the firing pin for the device, and placed it over the tail end of the flare container so that the firing pin was directly over the shotgun primer in the base of the flare. Then, holding the tube of the container in his right hand, he pointed it out over the water at about a seventy-five degree angle, and struck the bottom of the container a sharp blow with his left hand, wrist straight and locked.

The rocket-assisted flare arced out over the river with a loud whoosh, and burst several hundred feet above the water, the brilliant white flare suspended beneath the tiny parachute clearly illuminating the three sampans.

"Fire! Fire! Fire!" yelled Bromhead, as he pulled the butt of his M-14 tight against his shoulder and squeezed off three short bursts at the nearest sampan.

All along the point of the sandbar, firing erupted on either side of Bromhead as the rest of the ambush team began shooting. Their red tracers, one every fifth round, crisscrossed like some crazy Fourth of July fireworks show as they converged on the nearest boat.

The roar of the combined firepower of the ambushers was deafening. Bromhead had intentionally maximized the number of automatic weapons in the ambush party in order to achieve optimum effect. The noise of three M-14's, four BARs, and a .30-caliber M-1919A1 machine gun almost completely obliterated the flat staccato rattle of the M-2 carbines carried by the A-gunners.

The bullets chewed into the wooden hull of the sampan and it listed heavily to port and sank quickly in the shallow water.

As the first sampan began to sink, the men turned their fire on the second boat. There were a few sporadic rifle shots returned from the boat, and then a shattering explosion that temporarily washed out the light from the overhead flare. The second boat had been carrying either ammunition or explosives.

During the brief, eerie silence that immediately followed the spectacular destruction of the second boat, a new sound could be heard, a rapid put-put-put. Bromhead at first thought it must be some kind of light machine gun on the third boat, then recognized the sound for what it really was, an outboard motor. Although from its sound it was obviously of small horsepower, it nevertheless was pushing the third sampan downstream at a good rate of speed.

"Boom-Boom!" yelled Bromhead. "Hit 'em with the three-five!"

At the far left end of the ambush, Sergeant First Class Justin Tyme, the Green Berets' light weapons specialist, put down his M-14 rifle and grabbed the 3.5-inch rocket launcher that had been lying next to his foxhole. As he shouldered the weapon, the Tai striker in the next foxhole alertly jumped up and slid a rocket into the breach of the weapon. When the bazooka was loaded, he tapped Tyme on the helmet, signaling him that the weapon was ready to fire, and ducked quickly out of the way to avoid the back blast. Tyme lined up the ranging wires in the rocket launcher's sight on the bow of the sampan and squeezed the firing switch.

The rocket leaped from the tube with a roar, tore low across the surface of the river, hit the water once, skipped, and sailed neatly into the stern of the sampan. The high explosive charge in the rocket warhead ripped off the entire rear half of the sampan with an explosion only slightly less impressive than the one that had completely obliterated the second VC vessel.

"Downstream!" shouted Bromhead. "Try for the guide boat."

But as he shouted, the flare dropped into the river and spluttered out, plunging the men back into darkness.

Bromhead felt furiously for a second parachute flare and found one, but before he could fire it, there was a shuddering whir and two dazzling yellow-green flares popped overhead. Someone back at the camp had either heard or seen the firing, and unable to reach Bromhead by radio, had had the presence of mind to do exactly the right thing at the right time, firing two illumination rounds from the camp's 4.2-inch mortars, to light up the river.

It was the right thing at the right time, even though it was too late. As the flares burst, the sampan which had acted as guide for the others boats could be seen. It had put out into the channel as soon as the firing had started, and had doused its lantern. Two men could be seen in the stem, poling furiously, while a third tried frantically to start a small outboard. A fourth man could be seen farther forward, rapidly throwing wooden boxes over the side.

Tyme fired again, but the round was short, although not by much. The striker reloaded the weapon, but before Tyme could fire a third time, the sampan rounded the far bend of the river. A few seconds after it disappeared from sight, the distant putting of its outboard could be heard. Tyme stared disgustedly after the now invisible boat. It had been within range, and he'd been close enough with his first shot at it to feel confident that his second round would have blown it out of the water. But he hadn't got that second shot. He'd run out of time, pure and simple.

"Nice shooting, Boom-Boom," said a voice behind him. "How come you let that last boat get away, though?"

"Ah, I gotta get a bigger gun, that's all."

Tyme turned around. In the garish light of the flares, he could see the tight-lipped grin of Master Sergeant Anthony B. Fetterman, operations sergeant for the Special Forces A-team. For a second, he could see only the smile, despite the flares. Then he realized he was talking to the only bush on the sandbar. The bush came forward a step, and became Master Sergeant Fetterman.

"Nice costume," said Tyme. "Looks a little bit much for a beach party, though."

"Do you really think so? I thought it might be just the thing to add a touch of color to all this drab muck we've been wallowing in for the last five hours. Sort of like Mrs. Fetterman hanging a house plant in the crapper."

Both men laughed quietly, breaking the tension that all the men felt in the first few moments after a fight. The leaves on the front of the bush Fetterman had tied about himself were covered with mud. The only time more than a few twigs of the ambulatory plant were visible, was when the master sergeant rose up far enough in his foxhole to fire his M-14.

"Now I've seen everything," said Bromhead as a second pair of mortar flares glared over their heads. "A talking tree with a rifle. Can it walk too?"

"No. But it can dance," said Tyme. "I was just complementing Master Sergeant Fetterman on his originality and creativity in costume design. What do you think, should we give him the prize for most effective use of native materials?"

Bromhead took a step backward, as though to get a better perspective, and eyed NCO Bush critically.

"I don't know. Looks like it could be poison ivy to me. Maybe we ought to give it the signed Vallejo print for most natural appearance, and keep the autographed bottle of green label Pepsi for ourselves."

"I think before we do that, we ought to give the air force a call and have them defoliate it," said Tyme. "Unless we see it nude, how do we know it's a natural bush? It might be using Clairol."

"I think we should quit making jokes," said Fetterman, "and run a patrol down along the river for a klick or two and see if we can pick up any survivors along the bank. Besides, you'll notice that the bush is the only one of us with the necessary professionalism to maintain his cover at all times."

They laughed again; several of the Tai strikers laughed with them. Even though they did not understand what the Americans were saying, they knew from their mirth that it was supposed to be funny.

Bromhead shook his head and turned serious.

"I think we should take the men in and let them get cleaned up and get something to eat and some sleep. We're not going to find any survivors off the second boat, and probably none from the third. I don't know what happened to the guys on the first boat, but they didn't swim this way, and given the circumstances, I can't say as I blame them. Besides, it's dark, the cover along the river bank is heavy, and we just lost our second radio. There's no sense making ourselves targets for some wet, angry Charlie who might have managed to hang onto his weapon, and feels like becoming a hero of the revolution. We sank three VC sampans loaded with supplies tonight, and managed it without any friendly casualties. I think we should quit while we're ahead. Besides, judging from all the flares those guys back at camp are putting out, they must be dying of curiosity, and I'm dying for a drink."

The Fetterman bush shrugged its branches.

"The story of my life. All dressed up, and no place to go. All right, Lieutenant. I concede the logic of your argument. I'll take point, if that's okay with you, sir."

"Suit yourself, Master Sergeant. You in a hurry to get back for something?"

"Thought I might find a piece of nutcake in some of our C-rations for this damned squirrel, sir," said Fetterman in a very serious sounding voice.

"Squirrel?"

"Yes sir. Down here by my belt buckle. Furry little bastard keeps nibbling at my pine cones."

CHAPTER 2

SPECIAL FORCES CAMP A-555, ONE WEEK LATER

Captain Mack Gerber sat in the folding metal chair behind the makeshift desk in the tiny, tin-roofed, plywood hootch that served as his office, and watched the steam rising from the perforated steel plate runway that bisected his camp. It was a little after 0800 hours, and already it was hot.

Gerber rubbed wearily at his eye with his left hand, and reached for his coffee cup with his right. He'd lost track of how many cups of coffee he'd drunk since midnight, since last week, since coming to this stinking country. Half the *campesinos* in the Colombia must owe their jobs to him. He took a sip from the cup and swore.

"Goddamnit! Why the hell can't I get a cup of hot coffee around here? Everything's hot but the frigging coffee. The beer's hot, the milk, when we get it, is hot, even the goddamned air is hot. So why the fuck can't I get a hot cup of coffee?"

He looked at the cup. The surface of the coffee was steaming just like the surface of the PSP runway. He poked the coffee experimentally with his fingertip. It wasn't even tepid.

Gerber swore again at the coffee, snatched up the china mug, and contemplated hurling it out the door of the shack. He stopped himself just in time. China mugs were hard to come by out here. Instead, he dug his canteen out of his LBE, pulled the metal cup off the bottom of the canteen, and transferred the coffee to that. Gerber rummaged around in the butt pack attached to his pistol belt until he found the tiny, folding wing stove and a tube of hexamine fuel tablets. Then he stepped outside the hootch, knelt, and scraped a level spot in the dirt. He set the diminutive stove, really just an aluminum holder for the hexamine, in the level spot, and stood two of the fuel tabs on end in the center of it. Then he fished into the breast pocket of his jungle fatigues for a book of matches. The damp-proof army issue matches refused to light. Disgusted, he threw away the book after trying every match in it, and went back to his desk. He spent a full minute moving the papers and reports about until he found his Zippo underneath his .45 Colt Government Model pistol. The lighter was out of fluid.

Gerber repressed an urge to give the whole mess — stove, hexamine, and canteen cup full of cold coffee — a good kick across the compound. He sank back down in his chair and let out a long sigh.

"I've got to stop letting the small shit get to me like this," he muttered to himself. "I've got to get my mind off my personal problems and get on with the job."

He was interrupted in his musing by the sharp rapping of knuckles against the doorless frame of the hootch. It was Fetterman, his team sergeant, still clad in the black ninja suit he'd taken to wearing on night ambush patrols down to the river. At least, the top half of him was clad in it. He had on a pair of tiger-striped trousers, and was carrying an M-14 with bipod. Fetterman ordinarily carried an M-3A1 grease gun equipped with a sound suppressor on patrols, but lately he had opted for the heavier M-14 because of the greater range and penetration of its 7.62mm ammunition. There were places near the camp where the river was nearly 300 meters wide, and Fetterman had found the M-3 lacking in reach for punching holes in VC sampans running along the far bank.

"Come on in, Tony," said Gerber. "I didn't realize the patrol was back. How'd it go last night?"

"Not too hot sir. Charlie ran another convoy past us. Most of them slipped through before we knew they were there. Any idea when we're going to get some fresh batteries for the infrared scopes?"

Gerber shook his head.

"I spoke with Colonel Bates on the horn this morning. He's promised to see what he can do about expediting the supplies. Apparently something got fouled up and the batteries were misplaced coming through channels."

"Yes, sir. I suppose that is a more military sounding explanation than saying some bastard swiped them. Sir, we're going to keep missing the boat, so to speak, if we don't get those batteries."

"I know, Tony. So does Bates. He'll do what he can."

"Yes, sir. I know that, sir. The colonel's a fine man. I didn't intend any disrespect. If we had a few more like him in Saigon, and a few less like, well, like certain generals, maybe we could get on with winning the war."

Gerber gave him a weak smile. He understood only too well the sergeant's frustration, and his reference to certain generals. Brigadier General Billy Joe Crinshaw, deputy chief of operations of IV Corps, ultimately controlled the allocation of supplies to Special Forces A-detachments fighting in the Delta of South Vietnam, and Crinshaw didn't like soldiers who wore funny green hats. Not even ones who could get him good exposure from the gentlemen of the news media.

"We have any casualties last night?" asked Gerber.

"No, sir. I don't think the enemy had any, either. We might have damaged one sampan, but we didn't sink it. No way of knowing if it sank downstream. We'd have got a couple of them if we'd known they were there, but without infrared scopes, we're as blind as Charlie. Worse. He can keep in the shadows along the banks and have plenty of light to guide him down the river. We have to look across the surface, and try to see into the shadows on the other side. Without scopes, we can't see him until it's too late, and when we do see him, he runs away downstream, and we can't go after him because we've got no boats. That's what I wanted to talk to you about sir. Boats."

Gerber flashed him the weak smile again.

"Tony, give me a break. I can't even get batteries for the IR scopes, and now you want me to get you a boat? Would a PT do, or will you need a destroyer?"

"Please, sir, I'm serious. I've talked this over with Lieutenant Bromhead and Sergeants Tyme and Kepler. If we could get our hands on an eighteen-foot aluminum johnboat with about a twenty-five- or thirty-horse engine, we could run rings around those cruddy sampans. We could put four or five guys in it with M-fourteens or BARs, and mount a thirty-cal. machine gun up front. That way, if Charlie does manage to slip past us, we can run him down."

Gerber shook his head wonderingly.

"Who thought up this screwball idea?"

"Uh, I guess I did, sir, more or less."

"And Kepler and Tyme went along with it?"

"Yes, sir."

"And Lieutenant Bromhead liked the idea too, did he?"

"Yes, sir."

"Well, Tony, it looks like it's finally happened. My four best men have wigged out on me. Either that, or I've gone crazy. I can see it now, 'Sergeant Fetterman's Private Navy.' Crinshaw will go ape shit."

"Yes, sir. I suppose you're right at that, sir. Still, we figured it was worth a try. We're not having any luck this way. Besides, we figured it was just unconventional enough that we might catch Charlie with his pants down. And they did try to teach us to be unconventional at Bragg, sir."

Gerber stared for a second at the muddy, sweating, ninja-suited master sergeant, and almost broke out laughing.

"Yes, Tony, I guess they did try to teach us to be unconventional at Bragg, and right now, you look like their star pupil. Okay. I'm going into Saigon on Friday for a meeting with Colonel Bates, and I'll run the idea past him and see if it floats, but if he packs me off to some funny farm, you'll have to break in a new CO. Anything else?"

"No, sir. And thank you, sir. I'll have a written after-action report on last night for you as soon as I take care of my weapon and find some clean clothes."

"Find yourself some chow, too. And a couple hours sleep. The report can wait until after lunch."

"Thank you, sir. Oh, by the way, I fired up your coffee for you on the way in. Noticed it sitting outside the door. Probably's had the hell boiled out of it by now. You might want to get it before it cools off. If you can call this place cool, sir," Fetterman added.

"Thank you, Tony."

"You're welcome, sir."

"And Tony?"

"Yes sir?"

"You can call me Mack when it's just the two of us, you know."

"Yes, sir. Thank you, sir."

Fetterman turned and walked out.

Gerber sat behind his desk for a moment, staring after his team operations sergeant. Ninja suits and motorized johnboats turned into pocket destroyers. And that business a week ago when he came back in from the first night river ambush looking like a Christmas tree, all of them laughing about squirrels and pine cones. Maybe Fetterman was crazy. Maybe they all were. Maybe the idea was just crazy enough to work, and maybe Gerber himself was crazy for thinking it could.

Or maybe I really have gone insane, thought Gerber. I've lost my sense of reality, and imagined the whole thing. Fetterman was never here, talking about boats and outboard motors just now. He's still out with the patrol, and I'm sitting here with the weight of too many dead men, and too much responsibility for those still alive, resting on my shoulders.

Gerber shook himself out of it.

Tough luck, Mack, but there aren't any counselors out here in the bush, he told himself. Christ! If only I could hear her voice. Just for an hour talk to her. Be with her. Just for five minutes. Thirty seconds.

Bromhead came in with the bright orange mail pouch from Saigon brought by the morning supply helicopter.

"Anything for me, Johnny?" Gerber asked.

Bromhead dumped the mail on his own desk in the corner of the hootch, and sorted through it.

"Letter from your folks, and a flyer from something called Wiscon. Can't tell from the outside if that's a company or a tourist bureau. That seems to be it. Oh, yeah, there's a statement from your bank."

"Nothing from Nha Trang?" asked Gerber, unable to keep the combined note of hope and despair out of his voice. She was stationed in Nha Trang.

"No, sir," said Bromhead seriously. "Nothing from Lieutenant Morrow. I'm sorry, Captain."

Gerber nodded, and pretended to go back to reading a report on his desk. Bromhead couldn't help noticing that Gerber was holding it upside down, and had apparently already forgotten about the letter from his parents.

There is no sound so loud as a telephone that does not ring. No event so conspicuous by its absence as a letter neither written, nor received.

Bromhead wanted to tell his commanding officer that there was probably a good reason why she hadn't written, like too many casualties at the hospital. But there had been no letters from Flight Nurse Karen Morrow for nearly a month now. Bromhead couldn't think of anything to say that wouldn't sound hollow and false. He hesitated for a second, then picked up the rest of the mail and left to distribute it to the men. When Gerber finally realized he was holding the report upside down, and looked up, Bromhead was gone.

Belatedly remembering the coffee, Gerber went outside and retrieved his canteen cup. He poured the coffee into the china mug, watching the steam rise from its surface. When he tasted it, it was stone cold.

CHAPTER 3

B-TEAM HEADQUARTERS, SAIGON

Sergeant Derek Kepler shared the helicopter ride into Saigon with Gerber. Both men were unusually quiet, Kepler being occupied with the final preparation of his monthly intelligence estimate, and Gerber with a myriad of thoughts about improving the defenses of the camp, the increased VC activity in the area, and the mystery of the unanswered letters. At Hotel Three, one of the helicopter landing pads at Tan Son Nhut, the one which bordered the world's largest PX, they went their separate ways, Kepler to his meeting with the B-team S-2, Gerber to his meeting with Bates.

The administrative sergeant in Bates's outer office informed Gerber that the colonel would be a few minutes late, asked him to have a seat, and got him some coffee. Gerber failed to consider the possibility that the stuff might actually be warm, and burned his lip, nearly sloshing the coffee all over himself before he got the cup back under control. He had just settled back in his chair to cautiously enjoy the piping hot liquid when Bates came in.

"Morning, Mack. Taylor here taking good care of you? Sorry to keep you waiting, but we had some PITA Washington types come in this morning on a fact-finding tour. I've been over at MACV showing them where to look. Let's go into my office."

Once the door was closed, Bates didn't stand on ceremony. He waved Gerber into a chair and said, "So how's it going?"

"Less than spectacular, sir. Master Sergeant Fetterman took out an ambush patrol last night to work the river. They made contact, but didn't inflict any significant damage. Most of the VC convoy had already slipped past them, but they spotted a sampan and opened fire on it. I'm afraid we're going to keep missing opportunities until we get some new batteries for the IR scopes. We've tried improvising illumination, but that hasn't worked so hot. Flares and headlights let us see the river, but they also let Charlie know we're out there looking for him. He just sits back and twiddles his thumbs on the other side of the border until we get tired of the game, then runs a fast one past us."

"Headlights?" queried Bates.

"Yes sir. Sergeant Kepler scrounged some headlights from the base motor pool when he was here in Saigon a couple of weeks ago, along with a couple of truck batteries, and we've been using them as an improvised lighting device to illuminate the river. They work pretty fair, once contact is made, but like I said, if we use them for search, Charlie knows we're looking, and stays away."

Bates nodded. "Ingenious. I just hope Kepler didn't scrounge them the same way he did that ninety-millimeter recoilless rifle a few months back."

"No, sir. At least not the headlights. They'd all been scrapped out, replaced after the low beams had burned out. The high beam filaments were still intact, though, and that worked just fine for our purposes. I didn't ask him where he got the batteries."

"Mmm," Bates grunted. "It's probably just as well you didn't."

"Yes sir. I've sort of learned not to ask Derek too many questions about where he finds things. I don't suppose there's any word on when we might get those batteries for the IR scopes?"

"In this case, no news is no news," said Bates. "I've tried everything I can think of, but no dice. The batteries are officially misplaced somewhere in channels, and nobody knows where. I've put through another request, but of course, these things take time. It seems Supply is reluctant to give us any more batteries until they figure out exactly what happened to the last batch they sent us. Naturally, we're receiving the usual fullest cooperation from General Crinshaw's office concerning the speedy resolution of this unfortunate incident."

"Naturally," echoed Gerber. The usual fullest cooperation from General Crinshaw's office was none at all.

Bates was suddenly serious. "I have tried, Mack. Really. If there was anything I could do, I would. You know that."

"Yes, sir, I do. But a couple of my team members have suggested to me that there might be something else we could try. Something, ah, unconventional."

"Now, Mack, don't tell me you want to go over into Cambodia again. That's right out. It nearly cost both of us our jobs the last time you did that. I don't know about you, but I sort of like mine. It's not much, but it keeps the mortgage paid and the wife and kids fed. I was kind of thinking about trying to hang onto it, at least until retirement."

Gerber grinned. "No sir, nothing quite so dramatic. All we want this time is a boat."

"A boat?"

"Yes sir. Just a small one. Say about an eighteen-foot johnboat with a thirty-horsepower outboard."

"A johnboat?"

"Yes sir."

"With an outboard?"

"Yes sir. Something around thirty horsepower."

"What in the name of ham and lima beans for?"

"Well sir, without the IR scopes, we're having a hard time detecting Charlie's sampans before he slips through the kill zone. Double ambushes, one downriver from the other, are only partially successful. This way, we figure to bring the kill zone to Charlie."

"If I understand correctly what I think you're telling me," Bates began slowly, "you want me to find you an outboard motorboat, here, in South Vietnam, probably thousands of miles from the nearest marina, so that you can use it to go chasing up and down the Mekong after Viet Cong sampans?"

"Yes, sir. I believe you've got the gist of it."

Bates burst out laughing. He laughed until his eyes were watery, then wiped them on the back of his left hand. Finally he stopped laughing.

"I'm sorry, Mack. It's just that I had this sudden image of you in a blazer and yachting cap, chasing the Cong up and down the river. Mack Gerber's Private Navy. Crinshaw would love it."

"That's more or less what I told Sergeant Fetterman day before yesterday. Seriously, sir, it does make a kind of sense. Charlie has a real maneuver advantage over us in the river. With a boat, we can take that advantage away from him."

"Has it occurred to you that a boat is a poor thing to be in while Charlie is shooting at you?"

"Charlie shoots at us now, sir, when we can find him. Has it occurred to you how poor a place we're all going to be in if Charlie is allowed to continue his arms build-up unchecked?"

"All right. I'll see what I can do. We won't have anything in our TO&E except some rubber boats. Maybe we can talk the

Navy out of a barge or something. Now let's go over your operations reports for the last couple of weeks."

Sergeant Kepler found a very dejected Gerber when he stopped by the captain's billet in the VOQ at five p.m.

"Why the long face, sir?" Kepler asked. "Didn't things go well with the colonel?"

"Things went fine with the colonel, Derek," said Gerber, waving him into the single metal chair in the room as he sank down heavily on the army cot. "But Colonel Bates is only one man. He still can't get us the batteries we need for the IR scopes, he can't get Crinshaw to kick loose of those new AR-fifteen rifles he's got crated up down at the MACV warehouse, and he can't find us that boat that you and Sergeant Fetterman want so much. The only thing we've got in inventory is some rubber boats. The Navy wanted to loan us an LST for Christ's sake, provided we got MACV approval. The colonel told them no thanks, that we were interested in moving six to twelve men, not six to twelve hundred. Looks like the only way we're going to get a boat is steal one. If we can find one to steal, that is."

Gerber didn't mention that he had tried to call Karen in Nha Trang, but nobody at the hospital there seemed to know where she was. A personal problem was, after all, a personal problem.

"Well," said Kepler, "there it is."

"There it is," agreed Gerber. "Since we can't get a flight back until tomorrow, I suppose there's only one thing left to do."

"What's that, sir?"

"Let's go over to the club and get drunk."

"Uh, slight problem there sir. I'm the wrong rank, remember?"

"Christ, Derek, I'm sorry. I didn't think. Let's go downtown then. We can get a bite to eat at the Continental, then go over to the rooftop at the Caravelle and make fun of the journalists for a while, or just go hit a few bars. Unless you had other plans?"

"Sounds good to me, sir. Especially that first part. I'm getting a little tired of army chow. Besides, maybe having an officer along will keep me out of trouble," smiled Kepler.

It was an ironic jest, although neither man realized it at the time.

Dining at the Continental Hotel Restaurant proved to be a bit difficult, as the dining room host did not deem their wrinkled and sweat-stained jungle fatigues suitably formal for admission to his illustrious establishment. Gerber was already in a foul mood from the difficulties he was having getting the supplies he needed for his men, and, although he would not admit it to himself, he was irritated over the silence from Karen in Nha Trang. So he found his usually even-tempered demeanor slipping away in exasperation at the waiter's pomposity. Inexcusably, he was on the verge of punching the man in the face, when a light, restraining touch on his arm by Sergeant Kepler stayed his hand. Kepler had caught the eye of the maître d'hotel, and motioned him over. There followed a brief, whispered conversation in French, which Kepler spoke fluently, and the surreptitious exchange of what appeared to Gerber to be an inordinately large wad of piastres. They were led to a good table by the maître d', who removed a small reserved sign before seating them and motioned over a waiter to take their order.

Kepler, now operating in his second most favorite environment, ordered them each a double vodka martini, very

get some!" Everyone seemed to be looking at something off in the distance.

Kepler glanced questioningly at Gerber, who said, "Beats me what all the fuss is about. Want to go have a look?"

The two men finished the first of their drinks, and taking their second glasses firmly in hand, ambled over to the edge of the roof where the excitement was. Far away across the river, jets were flying a night airstrike somewhere toward Bien Hoa, the exploding napalm canisters producing brilliant red and yellow smears of color across the black night.

"Christ!" said one of the journalists. "I wish to hell I had my camera with me. Look at that."

"You bonehead," said another. "You'd need about a two thousand millimeter lens with an f-stop of one point four to get any of that from here."

"Yeah, man, I know. But just think what a beautiful picture I could get if I did. Somebody is really catching hell over there tonight."

Gerber and Kepler turned away. Both men had long ago ceased to be impressed with the technicolor nature of modern warfare. To them, all the pretty flashes that seemed to so delight the Saigon press corps meant only one thing. Somewhere out there, beyond the Vam Co Dong, men, soldiers like themselves, were dying in the darkness.

"Look, Captain," said Kepler, "I don't know about you, but when I drink, I like to get as far away from the war as possible. What say we get out of this overpriced joint and find us a place where we can buy an awful beer at a suitably low price?"

Gerber nodded his assent, and they drained their glasses and started for the elevator. As the elevator doors started to close, Gerber was startled to see a familiar form at the bar, talking to an air force officer. He could have sworn it was Karen, but just at that moment the doors snapped shut, cutting off the view. For a moment, he considered going back, then figured he must surely be mistaken and shrugged it off. It was, after all, a fairly improbable coincidence.

Once outside the Caravelle, Kepler moved close to Gerber and spoke in a low voice. "Sir, I don't know how to say this except to be blunt about it. Are you carrying a weapon?"

Gerber eyed his Intelligence sergeant with curiosity. "You know regulations prohibit us from carrying weapons downtown, Derek, or have you forgotten why we left our rifles back at Tan Son Nhut?"

"No, sir, I haven't forgotten, and you haven't answered my question. At the Intell briefing today, Lieutenant Simms, the B-team S-2, passed on the info that the Viet Cong are instituting a new program of assassination and terrorism aimed specifically at Americans. Embassy personnel and Special Forces are supposed to be priority targets. Since we are a bit distinctive, wearing these little green beanies of ours, I thought it might be a good idea if we were carrying a little insurance with us when we went wandering the streets of Saigon. So I'm asking again sir, are you armed?"

Gerber nodded slightly, feeling a bit self-conscious about the .45 Colt Government Model pistol he'd taken to wearing in a shoulder holster beneath his jungle jacket ever since arriving incountry. How could he realistically expect his men to abide by army regulations that he himself chose to ignore. "You?"

Kepler gave him a quick grin, dipped his hands into his own jacket pockets, and lifted them partway out, just enough to reveal a Walther PPK and a MK II hand grenade, stuck them back in his pockets.

"I can understand the pistol," said Gerber, "but isn't a grenade a bit much?"

Kepler shrugged. "Keeps me in balance. Otherwise I walk like Quasimodo."

"Okay," sighed Gerber. "Just don't forget and try to use it for a suppository. At least not while I'm around. Let's go find that beer."

They found a likely looking spot on Le Loi Street, a few blocks off Tu Do, with the improbable name of Dragon-In. It was only slightly more smoky than an HC grenade, and not quite so packed as a sardine can. There were a few other American uniforms in the crowd, but not many, which Kepler felt made it an unlikely bombing target for the VC, and meant the beer probably wouldn't be too overpriced.

They elbowed their way to the bar, Kepler in the vanguard, and he shouted something through the din at the barmaid, who shouted something back. Gerber shouldered himself into a spot next to Kepler, who bent over and shouted into the captain's ear in order to make himself heard above the stereo speakers that were blasting out American rock and roll with Japanese lyrics at a decibel level approaching that of a B-52 strike.

"Great bar, huh?" shouted Kepler. "We got a choice of two. What'll it be, Thirty-three or Tiger Piss?"

"No Ba Muoi Ba for me, thank you very much," Gerber shouted back. "I'd rather drink Tiger Piss."

Kepler smiled, nodded, and shouted to the barmaid. "Hai Biere La Rou."

The barmaid brought over two of the dark brown bottles with the red and yellow tiger's head painted on the front, and poured a glass for each of them. She waited patiently while they drank them down far enough for her to pour the rest of the beer. Kepler ordered two more before she carefully took the empty bottles away.

"They won't let you keep the bottles," Kepler shouted by way of explanation, "because they can't get any more since the French pulled out. They just keep refilling the old ones. If you try to take one, the White Mice chase you down and make you give it back."

Gerber nodded and sipped his beer. It was, at least, cold, and didn't taste nearly as bad as tiger piss. At least he assumed it didn't.

Several beers later, Gerber had completely forgotten about the excretion habits of tigers. He'd achieved that pleasantly warm buzz that comes just before the brain goes numb, and had even managed to temporarily forget about Karen Morrow, the air force flight nurse based at Nha Trang, with whom he'd fallen so desperately in love, and who lately had inexplicably stopped answering his letters. He'd even briefly forgotten Sergeant Kepler, who had somehow wandered off across the crowded bar, and was now deeply involved in conversation with a leg NCO. Judging from the quantity of "33" bottles in front of the leg, and Kepler's frequent gestures to the barmaid, the Green Beret had already bought the man a large number of beers and seemed intent on buying him several more. Gerber thought the procedure a bit unusual, as, to the best of his knowledge, Kepler was not given to fraternizing with rear area pogues. But they were carrying on like old buddies, so he assumed Kepler knew the man.

Gerber finally decided that he'd had enough beer for one evening; he waved to Kepler, who merely waved back and returned to his conversation. Gerber shrugged, made his way outside, and flagged down a passing Lambretta to take him back to the base.

In the morning, Gerber checked in with Colonel Bates's office before leaving for Camp A-555, in case there were any last-minute messages for him. There was a message, but not from the source he'd expected. A cryptic note from Kepler advised that he had "Returned to camp by other means, in order to ensure speedy arrival of specialized equipment."

Gerber had no idea what Kepler meant. He had requested no specialized equipment other than the batteries for the infrared scopes and the new AR-15 rifles, neither of which General Crinshaw seemed willing to make available.

Still puzzled by Kepler's note, Gerber took time to enjoy a long hot shower before leaving the VOQ, then stopped by the officers' club and bought four bottles of Beam's Choice to take back to camp with him. He wrapped the bottles carefully in his spare fatigues, and stuffed them in his pack. Then he bought four cases of Miller beer for his team and humped them over to Hotel Three to wait for his ride back to camp.

Gerber was nearly to the helipad when he tripped over a piece of loose tarmac and almost dropped the beer. In fact, he would have dropped the beer, had not a massive arm snaked out of nowhere and wrapped itself around the bottom three cases. Gerber was so startled by the unexpected aid that he nearly dropped the beer all over again.

"Here, sir, better let me give you a hand with that. You keep shaking it around like that, pretty soon there won't be anything left to drink but foam."

"Thanks," Gerber managed. The assistance had come from a young Special Forces sergeant who must have stood six feet seven if he was an inch, and was slightly less massive than an M-60 tank. He had close-cropped blond hair, thin blue eyes, and an open, friendly face with a boyish smile. He was dressed in full combat gear except for a helmet which hung from his pistol belt, was wearing his field pack, which looked ridiculously tiny on his huge frame, and had a duffel bag tossed nonchalantly over his right shoulder. He tucked the three cases of beer under his left arm, lightening Gerber's load considerably, and smiled again.

"Mack Gerber, A-Triple Nickel. Just going to the pad over there, supposed to have a ride coming pretty soon." Gerber couldn't believe he'd failed to notice the approach of this gentle giant.

"Then I guess you're the man I'm looking for. Sam Anderson, demolitions and light weapons. I'm your new replacement, which I guess makes me the team FNG. Hope you don't mind if I don't salute, under the circumstances."

"I'd be amazed if you could under the circumstances. From what Colonel Bates said yesterday, I didn't expect you for at least a week. What's the scoop?"

Anderson shrugged. "I'm just a buck sergeant sir. Nobody tells me anything, except when they're telling me everything. All I know is some personnel specialist back at Bragg said, 'Go,' and here I am."

"Great. I don't suppose they sent a commo specialist with you?"

"No sir. At least not so far as I know. You short one of them, too?"

"Just since May." Gerber didn't elaborate on what it had been like trying to run an A-detachment for nearly six months with only one communications specialist and one demolitions expert.

The flight crew finally arrived, and Gerber and Anderson shared the UH-1D ride out to Camp A-555 with three cases of claymores, two cases of M-16A1 bounding mines, and a great many cases of C-rations.

The ride back to camp was uneventful, although, as they were preparing to land, Gerber was mildly surprised to see a CH-47 Chinook lift off the runway that ran through the middle of his camp and clatter back past them in the direction of Saigon. To the best of his knowledge, no other flight had been scheduled into camp for that day. He hoped it wasn't a medevac flight, although he knew it was unlikely such a large aircraft would be used for that purpose.

Gerber was also mildly surprised to be met by Staff Sergeant Galvin Bocker when the helicopter landed. It wasn't all that unusual for whoever had the radio watch, usually Bocker, to come out and pop the smoke grenade for a helicopter to guide in on. But Gerber's team sergeant or executive officer was usually present as well, knowing their commanding officer would wish to be informed of the condition of the camp immediately upon his return. This time, neither Fetterman nor Bromhead were in evidence.

"Galvin, this small mountain here is Sam Anderson, our new number-two demolitions man. Sergeant Anderson, Staff Sergeant Bocker, our senior communications specialist, right now our only communications specialist," Gerber said. "Galvin, where the hell is everybody?"

"Sergeant Krung is on his way with a work party to unload the helicopter, sir. Sergeants Smith and Kittredge are out on a patrol with Lieutenant Bao. Sergeant Kittredge said he was getting kind of tired of spending all his time up in the FCT. I believe Sergeant Washington is doing a medcap with Sergeant Tam over at Ahn Tap today."

"I meant where's Bromhead and Fetterman? One of them is usually here."

Bocker looked uncomfortable. "I think you'll find them with Sergeant Kepler over by the ammo bunker, sir."

Somewhere in the back of Gerber's mind, a tiny alarm bell started ringing. "Uh, Galvin, he, uh, didn't come back in a dress again, did he?"

Bocker looked relieved. "Oh, no sir. Nothing like that. He hadn't even been drinking, sir. Well, he wasn't drunk anyhow. They're just looking over the new equipment."

"Okay. Fine. See to it that the beer gets taken over to the team house, will you?"

Gerber turned to Anderson. "If you'll come along with me, Sergeant, I'll introduce you to the rest of the team, then Sergeant Fetterman can show you where to stow your gear."

Anderson nodded and picked up his duffel bag as if it were an overnight case. After they'd gone a few steps, he asked, "Sir, if I'm not being out of line, what's this about Sergeant Kepler wearing a dress?"

Gerber considered not answering, then figured what-the-hell. Anderson was bound to hear the story sooner or later.

"Shortly after we established our camp out here, we decided we needed some heavier ordnance because there weren't any fire bases nearby. Sergeant First Class Kepler, our Intell specialist, went out and promoted a ninety-millimeter recoilless rifle and a hundred rounds of HE. He never did fully explain all the details, but he bribed a CH-47 crew with four bottles of Beam's to fly him, the ninety, and the ammo out here. When the chopper crew landed, Kepler was passed out in the back, propped up against a case of Beam's with his rifle in one hand and a bottle in the other, nattily attired in a nurse's uniform."

"Sounds like a right interesting sort of fella," mused Anderson.

Gerber shot Anderson a quick, slightly worried glance, and continued. "Well, come along and I'll introduce him to you."

As they approached the ammunition bunker, Gerber noticed a large squad tent had been erected near it. There was a fairly good-sized crowd of Vietnamese and Tai strikers gathered about the tent chattering excitedly. The strikers moved apart to let Gerber and Anderson through, and Gerber pushed aside the heavy canvas tent flap.

The Special Forces captain came up short. The tent was nearly filled by his A-team members, and by a large red and white object sitting upon a black steel trailer. Standing proudly before the trailer was Sergeant Kepler, who had obviously dressed with great care that morning — in the uniform of a lieutenant commander in the United States Navy.

CHAPTER 4

SPECIAL FORCES CAMP A-555

"What the hell is all this?" said Gerber without thinking, as Anderson bumped into him from behind. He moved slightly to let the new sergeant squeeze past.

"It's a boat, sir," Kepler answered brightly. "A sixteen-foot Starcraft vee-bottomed ski boat, with a seventy-five horsepower Chrysler outboard motor, and fold-down bench seating for six. Complete with three six-gallon gas tanks, a spare prop, and a tool kit with two spare sets of spark plugs. And, of course, a trailer."

"And a trailer," Gerber repeated slowly.

"Yes, sir. I figured we wouldn't want the boat without the trailer. It'd be too hard to handle that way."

"And would you mind telling me, Sergeant Kepler, or is it Lieutenant Commander Kepler, just what in the name of Sam Hill a sixteen-foot Starcraft, that was the word, wasn't it, ski boat is doing in my camp, with or without a trailer?"

"Certainly, sir. I stole it. Just like you said for me to."

Gerber was astounded. "I don't recall having ever seen this boat before, Sergeant. Let alone ordering you to steal it."

"No sir. I don't believe you have seen it before. I hadn't seen it myself until oh-five hundred this morning. But you did tell me last night that the only way we were going to get a boat out here was to steal one, and when such an outstanding opportunity presented itself, well, we do need a boat, sir, and I thought you'd want me to do the right thing."

Gerber felt suddenly ill. "How did you get it here?"

"Worked a trade with a Chinook crew. Gave 'em a case of Biere La Rou, a bottle of Beam's, two SKS carbines, an AK, and a Chicom Type 50 SMG."

"Where'd you get the Biere La Rou?"

"I bribed the owner of the bar we were in last night to let me steal it."

"And the weapons?"

"I let Sergeant Kepler have them from captured stock, Captain," said Fetterman. "They weren't in very good shape anyhow."

"You're in on this too, Tony? Damn it, you should know better. I might expect this sort of thing from Sergeant Kepler. He's been hanging around the CIA types too long. But you, you're a professional soldier. You should know that Army personnel can't just go around stealing motorboats whenever they feel like it and trading captured weapons to helicopter crews in exchange for carting the damned boats around Southeast Asia."

"It's only one boat, sir," said Fetterman. "And you're right, I am a professional soldier. And I was always taught that the first duty of a soldier is to close with and destroy the enemy. The boat will assist us in the performance of that duty. It'll do a hell of a lot more good for the war effort out here killing Cong with us, than it will towing some embassy fat cat and his mistress around the South China Sea on a pair of water skis."

"And just what are we supposed to do when the Navy starts asking what happened to their boat?"

"Sir," said Kepler, "it isn't the Navy's boat. It's got civilian registration numbers on it. The supply sergeant who told me about it said a Navy chief told him it was shipped over here as the personal property of some Saigon big shot at taxpayer's expense. The owner's got to have insurance on it, and I don't think he'd like the publicity he'd get if the story got out that he had it shipped over here on a U.S. Navy cargo vessel for his personal amusement, whoever he is.

"I'll admit that maybe I interpreted your wishes a bit too broadly, but we needed a boat, we couldn't get one through channels, and I found us a boat. I was careful, sir. Nobody can trace the boat here except the chopper crew who flew it out, and they don't know it was stolen. As far as they know, they ferried a questionable object for a generous naval officer. Besides, if they said anything to anyone, they'd get their ass in a sling for flying it out here in the first place."

Gerber threw his hands up in the air. "I give up. One of these days you guys are going to go too far, and we'll all wind up in Long Binh Jail. I suppose getting rid of it would cause more problems than stealing it did. At least you could hide the damned thing. There's a crowd of strikers lined up outside like this was a goddamned circus tent."

"We can keep the boat then?" Bromhead asked brightly.

Gerber shot him a withering look, then slouched his shoulders. He suddenly felt very old. What kind of crazy war was this?

"I don't give a damn what you do with it. Just get it out of my sight. And while you're at it, paint out those identification numbers."

He turned and stomped out of the tent, leaving Anderson to introduce himself.

By late afternoon, the once beautiful red and white ski boat sported a new paint scheme of olive drab and black tiger stripes that covered the outboard motor, dashboard, and even the steering wheel, as well as the deck and hull. The serial numbers had been filed off the motor, and half the windshield had been cut away to allow easy access to the .30-caliber Browning light machine gun, whose tripod had been bolted to the foredeck. Lieutenant Bromhead had wanted to mount one of the camp's .50-caliber machine guns on the bow, but had been persuaded by Sergeants Fetterman and Tyme that the recoil of the heavy weapon would tear its mount loose from the thin fiberglass deck. Fetterman and Tyme weren't sure the .30-caliber wouldn't do the same thing, but thought it less likely. A second .30-caliber machine gun was attached to a high, improvised mount bolted to planking wedged between the seats aft of the driver's seat. An M-79 grenade launcher and four bandoliers of 40mm grenades completed the basic armament of the little boat.

While the two sergeants and the lieutenant readied the boat for counterinsurgency operations, Sergeants Kepler and Anderson, assisted by LLDB Sergeant Suong, and Sergeant Krung and a work party from the Third Independent Tai Strike Company, labored at clearing a wide path from the rutted dirt road north of the camp down alongside the old, abandoned bridge to the water's edge, and constructing a small boat ramp and dock. Sergeants Suong and Anderson cut the necessary trees using detonating cord. These were then trimmed with machetes or hand axes, and lashed together or sunk into the river bed to form the dock. The ramp was accomplished in a similar fashion by lashing together several long tree trunks, anchoring the high end to other trunks driven into the bank, then weighing the lower end with large rocks, anchoring it to pilings driven into the river bed, and filling with earth.

By dark, both the ramp and dock were completed, and by twenty hundred hours, Bromhead and Fetterman judged the boat's paint to be dry enough to ask Captain Gerber's permission to take it out for a trial run.

There had been no sign of VC activity in the immediate area of the camp that day. Sergeants Tam and Washington had reported upon their return from Ahn Tap that some of the villagers had told them the Viet Cong were continuing to run supplies downriver. The village chief, who had befriended the Green Berets because of the good work they had been doing in his village for the last several months, reported that a large convoy of sampans was expected sometime within the next few days. Since this checked with intelligence from B-team headquarters in Saigon, gathered by CIA trail watchers and high altitude reconnaissance of Cambodia, that Kepler had been briefed on during his meeting with Lieutenant Simms the previous day, Gerber gave his permission.

At 2045 hours, Lieutenant Bromhead, accompanied by Sergeant Anderson, Lieutenant Bao, and Sergeant Phuoc, took a mixed Tai and Vietnamese patrol out through the wire and established themselves in their usual ambush position on the sandbar. Although there was a strong dislike among the Special Forces men for repeatedly using the same location, the sandbar was the only location which jutted out into the river, was reasonably close to the camp, and afforded a chance to bring effective fire on VC craft moving along the far bank.

At the same time, an all Tai patrol under Sergeant Krung left the camp by the north gate to check the path to the boat ramp for any booby traps the Viet Cong might have put there since dark, and to establish security around the dock and ramp.

Shortly thereafter, the boat was towed to the ramp by one of the camp's two jeeps, and after launching, was manned by Sergeants Fetterman and Tyme, by Sergeant Duc, who had replaced Sergeant Lim as senior LLDB communications specialist some months previously, and by Corporal Trao, one of the Vietnamese RF strikers who had become a skilled machine gunner, and who, unlike most of the RFs, was not afraid to go on patrols after dark. He had come originally from a small coastal village, had taken a keen interest in the motorboat when it arrived in camp, and had volunteered to man the machine gun in the bow.

Although Fetterman had started the outboard briefly during the day in camp to ensure that it would run, the men now left the motor off, so as not to give away their presence. Using long poles cut for the purpose, they pushed off, and allowed the boat to drift with the current, using both the wheel and the poles to guide it. After radioing their approach to Bromhead, they drifted past the ambush party and took up a position eight hundred meters downstream, and around the bend in the river from the sandbar. They anchored halfway between midstream and the opposite bank by lowering a large rock attached to a length of parachute cord off the bow. Bromhead then set his part of the ambush, and Fetterman's boat crew settled down to await the enemy.

The plan was for Bromhead to initiate the ambush as any VC sampans came past his position, illuminating the killing zone with Kepler's improvised headlight system. As the Viet Cong passed out of Bromhead's effective range by rounding the bend, he would then call for flare illumination of the whole area by the camp's 4.2-inch mortars. Fetterman would then cut the anchor line and move forward at high speed to engage the enemy on the water.

They did not have long to wait.

At 2320 hours, Sergeant Krung radioed from his position near the boat ramp north of camp that he had heard sounds in the river suggesting that boats were being poled downstream past the Green Berets' camp.

He could not be sure of the number of craft, as the boat or boats had been impossible to see without illumination because the sky was overcast.

Bromhead, being aware of the Viet Cong's tendency to run a scout boat ahead of their main supply convoys since the Special Forces had begun their program of riverbank ambushes, decided to let the boat or boats go by, if their passage could be detected, in the hope of a more lucrative target. He informed Fetterman of his decision, giving the master sergeant free rein to engage the vessel if it appeared likely to slip past him. He then cautioned Lieutenant Bao and Sergeant Phuoc to have their men hold fire and allow the scout to pass, unless the signal to open fire was given.

A few minutes later, Krung again radioed that he had heard a splash, followed by an angry whisper in Vietnamese to keep silent. Bromhead took this as evidence that he had guessed correctly that a scout boat was preceding the convoy, and advised Fetterman.

Five minutes later, Fetterman was horrified to see a lantern being lighted not seventy meters from his position. The VC vessel was directly in front of him. However, the kerosene light was swung back and forth a few times, and then extinguished. Their attention on signaling the other boats, the VC had apparently missed seeing the camouflaged motorboat.

Having been signaled by the scout sampan that it had safely passed the sandspit, known to be used as an ambush site by the soldiers from the nearby Special Forces camp, the other Viet Cong boats started downstream again. They had previously put into the far bank of the river upstream of the sand bar to await the all-clear.

Bromhead, unable to see the signal light because of the curving, vegetation-choked banks of the river, or to see more than a few dozen yards of its surface because of the darkness, could only wait what he hoped would be an appropriate amount of time, his ears straining for any sound that might indicate the passage of the boats.

Once he thought he could hear a faint swishing sound, like that made by the bow of a boat cutting through the water, but he heard it only briefly, and could not be sure that it wasn't merely wishful thinking on his part. Finally, unable to contain himself any longer, he reached out and connected the alligator clip to the twelve-volt truck battery that would activate the eight headlamps mounted on wooden stakes pushed into the soft sand in such an arrangement as to light up a wide area of the river in front of his men. He was rewarded by the sight of half a dozen sampans, either well into or just entering the killing zone, and at least two more already exiting it.

"Open fire!" yelled Bromhead. He pushed the safety on his M-14 forward and fired four short bursts at the boat directly in front of him, emptying the magazine of his rifle.

On both sides of him, two dozen men opened up, raking the boats with M-14s, BARs, Garand M-ls, and two .30-caliber machine guns. The Special Forces men and strikers had previously learned that submachine guns and carbines were impractical for this particular ambush situation, as they were lacking in both punch and range, particularly when the Viet Cong boats hugged the opposite bank, as they had recently learned to do. The A-gunners for the automatic weapons crews had had their M-l and M-2 carbines replaced by the heavier Garands.

Bromhead emptied four more magazines, firing in short bursts and changing magazines as rapidly as possible. He then grabbed up the handset of the PRC-10 radio, and called the camp. Bromhead had taken the time to wrap the radio in a heavy plastic garbage bag before leaving camp, and this extra precaution succeeded in keeping the radio dry and operating on the soggy sandbar.

"Zulu Operations, this is Nightstalker."

He was immediately answered by Sergeant Bocker in the base commo bunker. "Go ahead, Nightstalker."

"We have contact. Request pre-planned fire mission, ten rounds illumination. Fire on previously designated targets."

"Roger your request, Nightstalker. Stand by for shot."

Bromhead did not hear the final confirmation from Bocker that the flare rounds were on their way, for at that instant, the sandbar was raked along its entire edge by a sustained burst of machine gun fire from one of the sampans. The impact disintegrated the radio and missed Bromhead's face by only inches, knocking out two of the headlights as well.

The Viet Cong machine gun was joined almost immediately by a second, and a few moments later a third machine gun, firing from another sampan. Evidently, the VC, having grown tired of the repeated ambushes by the soldiers from Camp A-555, had beefed up the armament on their supply boats, equipping several of the sampans with RPDs. Although the ambush team was continuing to pour out rounds, the heavy automatic fire from the sampans was having some suppressive effect, and it was quickly becoming apparent to Bromhead that the low sandbar, devoid of any cover, was a less than ideal place to be.

Downstream, Fetterman was unable to wait for the flares from the camp's mortars before initiating his part of the action because of the close proximity of the VC scout vessel. As soon as he heard the firing from Bromhead's ambush team, he cut the anchor line and gave the order to fire on the enemy boat.

Corporal Trao and Sergeant Tyme immediately opened fire with the motorboat's two .30-caliber machine guns, firing in the direction the sampan was last seen, although it was no longer visible, having extinguished its signal lamp.

The automatic choke refused to function properly on the big Chrysler outboard, but Sergeant Fetterman had wisely taken the precaution of securing a piece of nylon parachute line to the choke, and was able to operate it manually. On the third try the engine caught, coughed, and then thundered into life. Fetterman immediately flipped the toggle switch on the dashboard that controlled the boat's single headlamp, and moved the throttle quickly, but smoothly forward. He intentionally did not ram it wide open because of the possibility of flooding the engine.

The headlamp flashed on, lighting a considerable section of the river, and revealing that the Viet Cong boat had drifted on its anchor line, and most of Tyme and Trao's shots had been wide of the mark. They immediately shifted their aim, and the two machine guns chewed into the flimsy wooden boat, riddling it with holes, and sending it quickly to the bottom of the river as the speedboat roared past it at a distance of about thirty-five meters.

Once past the enemy boat, Fetterman cut the power and put the wheel hard over to port, bringing his boat to a rapid stop crosswise in midstream. This maneuver had three important advantages. First, it kept the motorboat from rounding a curve in the river's path, thus keeping the presence of Fetterman's crew concealed from the sampans now fleeing Bromhead's ambush. Fetterman thought it unlikely that he had tipped his hand by sinking the scout, since the firefight raging at the sandbar would have masked Trao and Tyme's firing. Second, by staying on the downstream side of the curve, he kept his men clear of the fields of fire established for the troops under Bromhead, and would not endanger the ambush party with his own firing. Third, it put him in an excellent position to spring a second-stage ambush on the convoy as they came around a blind curve, with most of their attention focused toward the rear. It also, incidentally, afforded the opportunity to engage the enemy broadside, with automatic weapons fire, since Fetterman and Duc would be in position to lend their support to Tyme and Trao on the two .30-caliber machine guns.

Sergeant Duc immediately realized the significance of this, and swung the barrel of the heavy BAR he had brought along over the starboard topside edge, aft, near the engine. At the same time, he informed Fetterman that he had lost radio contact with Bromhead, although he was still in communication with the Special Forces camp, and that illumination rounds were on their way.

As the first of the flares broke overhead, casting the river and its jungle-lined banks into a garish nightmare world of sickly yellow-green, three sampans came into view around the bend.

"Fire! Fire!" yelled Fetterman unnecessarily, his shout lost in the roar of the two machine guns, Duc's BAR, and his own M-14.

Fetterman had taped three twenty-round magazines together, end to end. This arrangement made the rifle a bit awkward to handle, and Fetterman would never have done such a thing for a routine patrol because of the danger of getting muck and debris stuck in the inverted magazines. But he thought the modification outweighed the drawbacks in this situation, where the speed of reloading took on a greater importance, and there was little danger of getting foreign material into the magazines. Firing in quick, controlled bursts, he emptied one magazine at each of the boats, then snapped in a fresh magazine, letting the empty bundle of tape and metal stamping drop to the bottom of the boat. He jacked the operating rod of his M-14 to chamber a round from the new mag, then engaged the prop and raced the motorboat between the two nearest sampans.

As the motorboat passed between the Viet Cong boats, Tyme and Duc shifted their firepower to the port side, raking the boat on the left, while Trao concentrated on the boat on the right. Fetterman added his own fire to Trao's, shooting the M-14 one handed while he steered the motorboat. It was more a question of luck than accurate firing, but he had the satisfaction of seeing several of his own tracer rounds chew into the sampan.

Fetterman also saw several green and white tracers cross his own, as the VC in the starboard sampan returned fire, but it was sporadic, and both wide and high, and did no damage. Amid the hammering of the two machine guns and the deep-throated chugging of Duc's BAR, Fetterman recognized the rattle of an AK-47, possibly two, and the sharper crack of an SKS carbine.

Swinging the motorboat sharply about, Fetterman brought it back between the middle sampan and the third boat. While Duc continued pumping .30-06 bullets into the middle boat, both Trao and Tyme concentrated their fire on the third, as their original target was now screened by the middle sampan which had caught fire. The third boat abruptly exploded, showering the other three vessels with burning timbers from wooden packing cases and the hull of the sampan itself.

Upstream, Bromhead was having more than his share of trouble. It was apparent that the VC convoy was a large one, perhaps as many as a dozen boats, of which at least four were mounting light machine guns. These boats were also equipped with small outboard motors, probably not over five or six horsepower each, but enough to give them a good deal of maneuverability. As soon as Bromhead sprang his ambush, they had moved to take up positions between the sampan freighters and the sandspit and had returned a heavy volume of automatic weapons fire.

Bromhead was forced to redirect most of his firepower to deal with this threat, allowing the cargo-carrying boats to escape. Further, having lost his radio communications, Bromhead was unable to appraise Fetterman of the situation. In fact, had the radio not been destroyed, Bromhead would have used it to call down the camp's 81mm mortars on the river. He greatly regretted his decision not to bring a second radio so that he could carry more ammunition for the automatic weapons. Earlier, he had reasoned that the radios had proved less than reliable in the wet conditions prevailing on the sandbar, and he had no wish to lug along two worthless hunks of junk. Experience had indicated that duplication would not necessarily insure communications. For that reason, he had arranged a signal flare alternative for calling for illumination from the 4.2-inch mortars, and had taken only the one radio. He had made no provision for an alternative method of communicating the need for mortar supporting fire because he had not seriously considered the possibility of needing any.

Bromhead had equipped his ambush team with a 3.5-inch rocket launcher, since this had proven to be an effective weapon against the Viet Cong river traffic. Unknown to

Bromhead, however, the team of strikers handling the bazooka had been killed by the same burst of fire that had put the radio out of commission. LLDB Sergeant Phuoc, at great risk to himself, left the safety of his foxhole near the bazooka team's position, and sprinted fifteen yards under intense fire to the dead men, where, despite being wounded through one hand, he succeeded in getting the rocket launcher into operation; subsequently he sank two of the VC gunboats.

Sergeant Anderson, meanwhile, had put aside his M-14 in favor of an M-79 grenade launcher. His fire with the weapon was chillingly accurate, and after two very near misses, he succeeded in placing his third round directly on top of one of the two remaining sampans armed with light machine guns. The explosion from the 40mm grenade immediately silenced the machine gun mounted near the bow of the sampan, prompting the remaining gunboat to withdraw, and the damaged vessel sank a short time later.

"Jesus H. Christ!" said Tyme, as a flaming two-by-four-inch board whizzed by his head, following the explosion of the sampan. He ducked reflexively, although too late, but it was unnecessary. The six-foot-long timber missed his head by a good four inches. He glanced toward Fetterman and was surprised to see the master sergeant laughing hysterically.

"Are you all right?" yelled Tyme. "Are you hit?"

Fetterman nodded absently, and picked up something out of his lap. He held out his hand so Tyme could see. The explosion had blown a live, Soviet-made F-l hand grenade into the boat, and it had fallen in Fetterman's lap. It had not exploded, however, as the safety pin was still in place.

The middle sampan had been heavily damaged by the concentrated fire from the motorboat, and was adrift and burning fiercely. Its crew was killed, or had abandoned it. Fetterman brought the ski boat around smartly, in order to attack the remaining sampan which was listing badly but still manned and afloat.

Just then, five more cargo sampans came into view, escorted by an armed sampan, and a pitched gun battle developed. Although the crews of the cargo-carrying boats seemed to be armed mostly with a collection of rifles and carbines, the VC gunboat's machine gun was a definite threat. The fiberglass hull of the Starcraft offered no more in the way of protection than the wood of the sampans.

"Fetterman, get us between some of the sampans before that fucking MG chews us up," yelled Tyme, hosing down two of the nearer boats with his machine gun. "Duc, break out the M-79 and get some grenades on that mother."

Fetterman put the wheel back over hard, intending to run the ski boat directly between the two sampans Tyme had machine gunned. As he did so, a burst from the RPD struck the rear of the Starcraft and the engine sputtered and died. The burst also struck Sergeant Duc, knocking him backward onto the deck.

Flares from the camp's 4.2-inch mortars were popping steadily overhead. As the motorboat came off plane and settled back into the water, losing its forward momentum, Fetterman steered for the slot between the two sampans. Then, as the boat drifted forward, he realized the engine had been hit, and he abandoned the wheel. He grabbed his M-14 again and began firing at anything that still moved in the two boats, leaving Trao and Tyme to deal with the RPD.

"Fetterman! Take the Browning." Tyme dropped the grip of the .30-caliber and scrambled for the M-79 that the wounded Duc was still trying to get loaded. Scooping up the grenade launcher, he shoved the round into the breech, aimed at the

Viet Cong gunboat, and fired. The 40mm grenade blooped out of the tube, and Tyme loaded and fired three more times without waiting to see where his first round hit, snatching the grenades from Duc, who held them out to him left-handed. The second and fourth rounds hit the sampan, destroying it utterly.

While Tyme had been busy with the M-79, Fetterman had succeeded in having a deleterious effect on the RPD gunner's aim with the .30-caliber machine gun. As soon as he saw the first of Tyme's grenades hit just under the bow, knocking the VC gunner into the water, Fetterman shifted aim to the nearest of the other sampans. The full metal-jacketed bullets chewed through the wooden hull like angry termites and ripped the boat apart like it was made of rice paper.

Despite all efforts, the other three sampans succeeded in escaping downstream, although Tyme continued to lob grenades after them with the M-79 until they were out of sight, achieving several near misses.

Fetterman had several belts of ammunition linked together to allow the Browning machine gun to maintain sustained fire. One of these broke, and the remaining ammunition in the belt clanked to the bottom of the motorboat amid the tinkling of spent brass, and the firing ceased. In the abrupt silence that followed, broken only by the crackling of the burning sampan, Fetterman became aware that his was the only machine gun that had been firing for the last several seconds. He glanced quickly forward, where Trao was manning the bow machine gun.

There was a large wet blood spot on the foredeck between the machine gun mount and the boat's horn, and a neat round hole through the remaining half of the windshield. The bullet's path would have taken it directly through the back of

Fetterman's head, had the master sergeant still been seated behind the wheel. But Fetterman had not been in the bullet's path. Of the little Vietnamese corporal who had shown such keen interest in the boat and volunteered for the night's mission, there was no other sign.

By the dying light of the last of the camp's flares, Fetterman stared at his own reflection in the sticky black pool. Then the flare dropped hissing into the water, and the image faded out, leaving only the distant crackling of the drifting, burning sampan.

"That's pretty much it, Captain," Fetterman was saying. "We called and paddled around for probably twenty minutes, but we never did find him. Finally, we had to break off the search. Sergeant Duc was wounded and we had to get him medical attention. We beached the boat and linked up with Lieutenant Bromhead. He sent Lieutenant Bao and some of the strikers back to find the boat and see if they could tow it back to the dock by hand."

"How is Duc?" Gerber asked.

Fetterman shrugged. "He'll pull through I guess. The bullet entered his shoulder and lodged in his back, but it missed the lung. Doc McMillan said it shattered his collarbone. His flak jacket stopped two other rounds. If it hadn't, he'd be dead for sure."

Gerber turned to Bromhead. "How about your casualties, Johnny?"

The three men were seated in the tiny hootch that served as Gerber's office. A bottle of Beam's Choice sat on the desk of ammo crates between them, and Gerber reached for it to pour each of them a second drink.

"Two dead, two wounded, Captain. We lost two strikers, probably the best bazooka team we had among the RFs. Sergeant Phuoc's hand is pretty fucked up, but he's still got all his fingers. If it doesn't get infected, he probably won't lose it, but McMillan isn't taking bets on how long before he can use it again, or how much. One of the Tai's got shot right through both cheeks, but he's still got his teeth. At least he's got as many as he had to start with."

Gerber nodded and took a sip of his Beam's, letting the smooth liquid roll down his throat. "Estimated damage to the enemy?"

"Between the two ambushes, we sank nine boats for sure, and may have sunk another. I figure we damaged another three or four. Enemy casualties, well, I don't know. Figure two or three to a sampan. How many killed and how many wounded? I just don't know. We didn't capture any, and we didn't see any swim ashore. We definitely destroyed four automatic weapons, probably more if you want to count AKs, although I don't think they had too many of those. My team cooked off one boatload of ammo, and from the way Sergeant Fetterman describes the explosion, I'd say we can credit a boat of demolitions material and grenades. Beyond that…" he shrugged. "The river's ten, fifteen feet deep in places out there, this time of year, and although the current isn't strong, it is constant. We might be able to get a better idea in the morning, but I wouldn't count on it."

"Okay, you guys get cleaned up and get some sleep. In the morning we'll send a patrol downriver to see if we can find anything. In the meantime, I'll try to figure out how we're going to write up an after-action report on this thing without admitting that we utilized a boat Kepler stole because he thought I wanted him to get us one."

After Bromhead and Fetterman had left, Gerber poured himself a third drink, and sat as his desk wondering where he'd gone wrong. He'd been a good soldier. Won a Silver Star and two Bronze in Korea as an enlisted man, and picked up a Purple Heart. Afterward, he'd gone to the University of Iowa on the G.I. Bill, earning a commission as a second lieutenant through the Army's ROTC program the same day he earned his bachelor's degree in botany. Having already been a paratrooper, he found his way into the Special Forces fairly naturally, especially after coming out on the losing side of a bar fight most unbecoming of a junior officer and fledgling gentleman, in Bad Tolz, West Germany. The fight had started because of some derogatory comments about second lieutenants made by some U.S. Army soldiers wearing funny hats.

Now Gerber wore the same funny green hat. After losing the fight, earning a green beret had been the only way he could think of to prove to those soldiers that he was as good as they were. The fact that it had been eight-to-one odds was something Gerber had considered insufficient to prove his point, even if four of them had required hospitalization afterward. The fight had been a wild and crazy thing to get into, but one of the soldiers had thrown the first punch. Gerber had merely retaliated in kind. Besides, although he didn't like to admit it to himself, there had always been a bit of the mustang in Mack Gerber.

That was why he had enlisted in the army right after high school, and why he had volunteered for the paratroops, and later Special Forces, and later still for Vietnam. That was why he put up with a team sergeant who affected ninja suits and fancied exotic weapons and seemed to like combat just a little bit too much, and an Intell sergeant who had a penchant for trying on women's clothing, and stealing little things like truck batteries, 90mm recoilless rifles, and sixteen-foot, six-passenger vee-bottomed ski boats. That, and the fact that both men were damned good at their jobs.

But something was gnawing away at him, and although Gerber knew that his deteriorating relationship with flight nurse Karen Morrow was a large part of it, he knew that it wasn't everything. He was a young man, barely pushing thirty, and he felt older than the Vietnam hills. Part of it was the constant strain of the day by day fighting of an often brutal, sometimes senseless war; even Korea seemed sane by comparison. Mostly it was the frustration of not being allowed to win a war he knew was winnable. The constant struggle with Saigon for the most elementary equipment and supplies, the Army's restrictions on employing the very tactics the same army had taught him were necessary to fight a counter-guerrilla war and win it, the constant political battles with General Crinshaw at MACV, whose only purpose in life seemed to be creating misery for Gerber and his men, and who seemed to consider all of Special Forces a personal affront, these were the things that galled him most.

Here I am, thought Gerber, getting ready to make up an after-action report. I've got to lie to my CO about an operation in which we killed or wounded twenty to thirty Cong, sank or destroyed five or six tons of supplies, and deprived the VC of four machine guns and ten river transports, with a loss to our side of only three friendlies KIA and those WIA. I can't admit to him that in order to do the job we had to steal a goddamned boat since we couldn't get one through channels, because people like Crinshaw don't know there's a war going on out here. They think it's all some kind of goddamned game, just a bunch of people dressed up in cute little soldier suits, playing at war. Pow! You're dead! No I'm not! You can't do that because Mom said. Because the president said, or congress said, or Jane-Fucking-Fonda and world opinion said, no you can't do it that way, now be a good little boy and play by the rules. Christ! The whole fucking mess makes me sick of it.

"So why don't you do something about it?"

"What?" Gerber started.

"Whatever it is that's eating you, Captain."

A startled Gerber jerked his head up and glanced at the doorway of the hootch. Framed in the sandbagged casement stood a man.

He was dressed in a set of jungle utilities and a floppy boonie hat, all of which had been died black. He was wearing black issue boots, black gloves, and a set of black VC web gear, and had an M-60 machine gun slung over one shoulder. The metal body of the gun had been camouflaged with bits of black electrical tape.

The whole costume was so reminiscent of one of Fetterman's outlandish garbs, that it was a half-second before Gerber realized the man was not his team sergeant. Fetterman had worn tiger stripes tonight. To match the boat, he'd joked. Besides, the master sergeant had just left with Bromhead, and the camp had no M-60s. This fellow was much taller than Fetterman. And thinner, if that were possible. He was so gaunt, in fact, that he looked positively emaciated. A poncho-liner blanket hung loosely from one shoulder of his web gear like a cape, partially covering the machine gun.

The man stepped forward slightly, and Gerber studied his face. It was a dead, pasty white, the color of some corpse that had been left in the water too long.

Christ, thought Gerber. It's three o'clock in the morning, and this guy is wearing sunglasses.

"Count Dracula, I presume. Tell me, Count, you're a little late for Halloween, aren't you?" said Gerber.

"Not bad, Captain. Most people can only manage 'Who the hell are you?'"

"All right, I'll bite," said Gerber. "Who are you and what are you doing in my camp?"

"That's easy, Captain. I'm Schmidt, Vladimir T., Sergeant, U.S. Army Special Forces. I'm your new commo specialist."

"Well I'll be go to hell," Gerber swore softly.

"Very probably we'll all be, Captain. Very probably we'll all be."

CHAPTER 5

B-TEAM HEADQUARTERS, SAIGON

In the end, Gerber decided to prepare two reports on the night's action against the Viet Cong supply convoy. One was for official consumption and described the events in terms of a double riverbank ambush; the second, which he intended to give to Colonel Bates, detailed the true nature of the operation against the sampans.

After he'd completed the two reports, he'd had just enough time to grab a shower and shave, wolf down a quick breakfast, and catch the morning supply helicopter back to Saigon. He intended to deliver the report in person to Bates. Gerber was going to be completely candid with his commanding officer. He had learned that he could trust Bates when he had supported Gerber's decision to mount an illegal operation in Cambodia in order to disrupt a massive build-up of Viet Cong troops preparing to assault Camp A-555. The operation could have cost both men their careers. Instead, it saved the camp.

Now, Gerber hoped that with the proven effectiveness of small craft to interdict Viet Cong river traffic, as detailed in the report, Bates would be able to approach the right people through unofficial channels to get them issued a couple of boats officially. They would then be able to officially prove the worthiness of the concept, and get the Saigon command structure to take a look at it. Gerber was already convinced that river-borne patrolling of Vietnam's extensive system of rivers, waterways, and canals could be an enormous aid to the disruption of communist supply lines and the entire war effort. However, he knew that Bates was still an army career officer, with a strong sense of what constituted proper military behavior, albeit tempered with a sense of combat expediency, and he was not altogether sure how the colonel would react to the revelation that they had stolen a boat. Thus, he approached Bates's office with some trepidation.

"Morning Sergeant Taylor," said Gerber, opening the door to Bates's outer office. "Is the Colonel in?"

"Good morning, sir," the administrative NCO answered "He's in his office. Did you have an appointment?"

Gerber shook his head. "Just need a quick word with him. Tell him it'll take about five minutes, ten tops."

The sergeant picked up the telephone from his desk, spoke briefly, then motioned Gerber to go on in.

"Hello, Mack. Doing a little rear area goldbricking? I thought you'd gone home."

Gerber gave him a weak smile. "I wish I could go home, if by that you mean The World. If you mean back to camp, I did go. Yesterday."

"So what are you doing in my office today?" asked Bates, puzzled.

"We ambushed another VC supply convoy coming downriver last night, and sank nine boats. We damaged several others, one of which was later found beached and abandoned."

"Congratulations." Bates, sensing something more, asked suddenly, "Casualties?"

"Light. Three RFs KIA, two Tai strikers and an LLDB Sergeant wounded. It's all detailed in the report I've brought."

"So what's the problem, then?"

Gerber took a stack of papers out of his green canvas briefcase and laid them on the colonel's desk. "There are two copies of the report. The one on top is the official version. I think maybe you'd better read the one on the bottom first."

Bates read the report through carefully without comment. When he finished, he looked up and asked just one question. "Tell me, Mack, where did you get the motorboat?"

"Sergeant Kepler found it for us, sir."

"I see," said Bates in a level voice. "And am I to presume that Sergeant Kepler 'found it' in his normally resourceful manner?"

"I'm afraid so, sir. Sergeant Kepler was aware of our critical need for a boat. He was one of my men who first suggested it as a possible solution to the VC sampan problem. And, uh, well sir, when a boat just sort of presented itself that seemed tailor made to our requirements, he... well sir... that is... well, he said he thought I'd want him to do the right thing. Sir."

"Your Intelligence sergeant seems to have kind of a curious sense of right and wrong. Maybe you ought to have a little talk with him about it."

"Yes sir. I've been meaning to do exactly that, sir."

"And while you're at it, you might tell him to get the boat out of your camp."

"Yes sir. I'll tell him to get rid of it."

"I didn't say get rid of it, Mack. I just said to have him get it out of your camp. Take it somewhere outside the perimeter and camouflage it."

"Sir?"

"Mack, there's no sense in throwing out the baby with the bath water. If I thought it would increase the number of Cong and supplies your men are taking out by anything close to what you did last night, I'd go out and steal a battleship. The idea of a mobile, river-borne ambush team is one of the best I've heard of. I'll admit I had some doubts at first, but your report proves the validity of the concept. I just don't want you guys to get caught red-handed by Crinshaw."

"What's General Crinshaw got to do with..."

Bates snorted and broke into a mischievous grin. "You mean you really don't know? I think you'd better tell Kepler to be more careful next time about whose boat he steals."

"Oh my God. You don't mean that it's..."

"None other. Shipped over here at great expense to the American taxpayer, no doubt. It seems General Crinshaw is a fan of water-skiing. Won a few trophies for it in his younger days, I believe. He went down to the docks late yesterday morning to admire his boat, and found out it was missing. He was not amused."

Gerber didn't know whether to laugh or cry. "How did you find out? Are you sure?"

Bates chuckled. "My spies are everywhere. The General's Admin NCO and mine are old drinking buddies. Mine, however, has developed the ability to open his ears instead of his mouth when he's drinking. Very convenient at times. Unless two vee-bottomed, sixteen-foot Starcraft ski boats came up missing from the Saigon docks yesterday, I'm sure. I hope you at least had the good sense to file off the serial numbers."

"And paint it, add two machine gun mounts, and cut off half the windshield. Under normal circumstances, I don't think I'd recognize it as the same boat. Unfortunately, I believe we can assume that General Crinshaw would. I think I'd better take your advice on getting it out of my camp."

"I think that might be wise," said Bates. "In the meantime, I'm having dinner and cocktails with General Hull this evening. As you know, the General has an interest in Special Forces, and has been fairly supportive of our organization in the past. It's amazing what earning a pair of jump wings can do for the attitude of a career officer. Anyway, I intend to bring up the idea of river patrol boats with General Hull. If he's receptive to the idea, I may show him your report. If not, I don't think it would be wise to push the issue at this time, given the complication of explaining how you got the boat."

"Thank you, sir. I appreciate your discretionary judgment in the matter."

"No sweat. Just don't tell Kepler you need a typewriter. He's liable to help himself to Sergeant Taylor's, and I can't type worth a damn."

"I'll be sure to tell him your office is off limits, sir," grinned Gerber.

"Fine. I also plan to mention to General Hull that we've been having a little trouble with our supply line. Yours isn't the only camp that's been having difficulty getting what it needs, although you do seem to have more trouble than the rest of them. I've got to be careful not to make too big a deal of it, because we don't want to alienate Crinshaw completely. But I am getting a little tired of playing his games, and it's just possible that a low-key inquiry from General Hull's office might be all the nudge that's necessary to get things moving again."

"Thank you, sir. And while I'm at it, thanks for the replacements. It's nice to have the team up to full strength again."

"Replacements? What replacements?"

"Anderson and Schmidt, sir. I picked up Anderson at Hotel Three yesterday, and Schmidt came in last night."

"I know about Anderson, although I didn't know he'd arrived. Who in the hell is Schmidt?" Bates seemed genuinely perplexed.

"The new junior commo guy. A little on the weird side, but then, most of my men are a little idiosyncratic. Seems to know his stuff, though. Bocker checked him out on the radios last night — well, early this morning. He came in around zero three hundred."

"He came in from where? Patrol?"

"No, into the camp. He arrived then."

"How?"

"What do you mean, how? Helicopter I suppose. I was working in my hootch on that report after Bromhead and Fetterman came in from the ambush, and he showed up at the door. He had his travel orders with him."

"Hmmm, weird," mused Bates. "As far as I know, we didn't have any choppers out last night. It was a pretty quiet night. A-557 took some rocket fire, and A-552 drew its usual half-dozen mortar rounds, but that's about it, except for the action up your way.

"Anyway, I didn't know he was here, or even en route," finished Bates. "It must be some foul-up in Personnel. Just one more thing to go wrong. I'll have Taylor check it out when he gets a chance.

"Anything else I can do for you today?"

"No sir. I don't think there's anything else you can do."

Bates detected the subtle nuance. He'd thought something was bugging the man during their meeting the day before yesterday. It wasn't anything definite, just a vague uneasiness, a sort of intuitive feeling that all was not well with his favorite A-detachment commander. It wasn't anything he could put his finger on; he'd finally chalked it up to frustration on Gerber's part over the inability to get the supplies he needed for his men, particularly the replacement batteries so desperately required for the camp's four infrared night vision scopes. Now he suspected difficulties of a more personal nature. Bates, however, had never claimed any great fame to clairvoyance, but that annoying feeling of something wrong was persistent. He decided that the best way to deal with the situation, like most tasks, was to confront Gerber directly.

"Sit back down a minute, will you Mack? Let's talk."

Gerber did as requested.

Bates held out a slim case. "Cigarette?"

Gerber shook his head and Bates lighted one for himself, took a puff, then rubbed his forehead with the back of his thumb.

"Look, I don't mean to be a nosy old bastard, but anything that affects the performance of my men concerns me. It has to, because of the nature of our jobs. Now, I get the distinct impression that you're one unhappy fellow about something. Want to tell me what's bothering you? Off the record if you like."

Gerber was mildly surprised at Bates's perceptive insight. He hadn't realized it showed. "It's nothing, sir, just a few little personal problems. It won't affect my job performance."

"Maybe it will, and maybe it won't. It's already affecting you. I can see it, and if I can see it, others can. The boys in the field have got to have complete confidence in their CO. If they get to worrying about what's happening to the boss, they're liable to be wondering how he's going to react in a combat situation when they should be reacting themselves. We lose people that way, Mack, and I don't want to lose any of my men. Not any of them."

"Are you saying some of my men have expressed a lack of confidence in me?" asked Gerber stiffly.

"No. Of course not."

"Are you saying you've lost confidence in me, then?"

"Come on, Mack. You know better than that. Look, this is old Al Bates you're talking to. How long have we known each other, anyway?"

"Since Korea, sir."

"Knock off that sir shit. I'm trying to help. Now why don't you get it off your chest? You'll feel better, and I'll stop pestering you. Now what is it? Financial trouble? Problems at home?"

"No, nothing like that. Mom and Dad are fine."

"Your brother?"

"Doing great in school. I think he finally realized he'd better study if he wanted to get into college next year."

"So what the hell is it, girl trouble?"

Gerber felt a bit embarrassed. "Something like that."

"I see. Who is it, that nurse you've been seeing?"

Gerber nodded slightly.

"Is it serious?"

Gerber let his head drop into his hands and rubbed his eyes. "Who knows? I thought it was. I thought she did too. Now I don't know. I write, she doesn't write back."

"You tried to call her?"

"Several times. Nobody up at Nha Trang seems to be able to find her. I don't know if she's avoiding me, or what."

"You sure you're not reading more into this thing than is there? You know how these wartime romances can be."

"I'm not sure of anything anymore, except that I love her and I want her in my life."

"Okay. You go take care of whatever other business you've got and get some lunch. Come back here at thirteen hundred. I've got a meeting over at MACV this afternoon, but I'll leave travel orders and an authorization for a three-day incountry R and R with Taylor out front. You go up and see this young lady, straighten out your problems with her, and then get your butt back out to your camp and your mind back on business, all right?"

"Yes sir. Thank you, sir."

"Okay. Now stop cluttering up my office, will you?" said Bates gruffly. "I've got tons of paperwork to do, and Sergeant Taylor assures me that each piece is vitally important to the war effort."

Gerber stood and saluted. "Thank you again, sir."

Bates returned the salute. When Gerber had his hand on the door knob, Bates said, "You know, Mack, you don't have to call me sir when it's just the two of us."

Gerber turned. His face broke into a wide grin.

"What's so funny?" asked Bates.

"Nothing sir. Just thinking of a conversation I had with my team sergeant a few days ago. Thank you." He opened the door and walked out.

CHAPTER 6

8TH FIELD HOSPITAL, NHA TRANG

When Gerber had arrived in Nha Trang, he'd gone first to the Special Forces compound there, to see if there were any messages for him. The brief communication he'd sent to Bromhead from B-team headquarters in Saigon must have drawn some puzzled frowns upon its receipt at Camp A-555. It had simply advised Lieutenant Bromhead that Gerber would be in Nha Trang for a few days, and had included a message for Fetterman advising him to "Relocate special equipment due to possible hazard of flying brass landing in its vicinity." The message had provoked a query from the camp to repeat the contents, and the B-team radio operator had done so. Gerber had been unable to wait for an acknowledgment because he'd had to run to catch the Army Aviation Caribou bound for Nha Trang.

At the compound, however, Gerber got the confirmation he'd hoped for. There were two messages. The first, from Bromhead, acknowledged Gerber's announced absence from the camp. The second, from Fetterman, was a bit more cryptic.

It read, "Assuming I understand your warning about possible hazard to special equipment from high-flying brass, I have relocated same to less secure area."

The two key terms in the message were Fetterman's changing of flying brass to high-flying brass, letting Gerber know that he had understood the word to be a reference to the Saigon command structure, and not ammunition casings, and the statement that the special equipment had been relocated to a less secure area, meaning the boat had been moved outside of the camp.

With the possibility of General Crinshaw dropping in on his camp and discovering the mutilated motorboat no longer hanging over Gerber's head like the sword of Damocles, the captain left his gear at the TOC for Special Forces operating out of Nha Trang. The center would be staffed round the clock, and he would be able to pick up his things at any time. Gerber then promoted a jeep, and drove to the hospital.

Inside, he wandered around until a nursing supervisor told him where Karen's ward was. He went there and wandered around some more until one of the nurses told him Karen had worked a double shift last night, and was probably sleeping in her quarters. Gerber put on his best, honest face, and asked how he could find that. Evidently, he came across as sufficiently trustworthy, and the nurse told him where to go.

Gerber found what he hoped was the right room, and knocked. He was answered by silence, but the corporal, or airman, or whatever she was, downstairs at the desk, had said Karen was signed in, so he tried again, a bit louder. Finally, he heard a faint voice.

"I'm sleeping. Go away."

Gerber smiled, and knocked louder.

"I'm dead. Now please go away."

Gerber, grinning broadly, pounded on the door with both fists.

"All right, Goddamnit! I'm coming. But this had better be pretty damned important or somebody's going…"

She yanked open the door.

"Mack! Uh, I was just sleeping. What are you doing here? That is… I mean… hi."

"Hi yourself. Are you going to invite me in?"

"What? Oh, yeah, sure. Come in. I'm sorry. I just woke up and I'm not thinking very well."

"You already said that." Gerber moved into the room and took a seat in the single, folding metal chair. It was, he reflected, almost a carbon copy of the room he'd had in the BOQ at Tan Son Nhut.

Karen closed the door and shuffled across the floor to collapse on the bed. "What are you doing here?" she asked, rubbing her eyes.

"Silly question. I came to see you, of course."

"Just like that?"

"Well, not exactly. I was in Saigon on business. Colonel Bates decided to give me a three-day incountry R and R, and here I am. I hope I'm mistaken, but you don't seem very pleased to see me."

"Of course I'm pleased to see you. It's just that I'm tired and well, I wish you'd called first. That's all."

"I tried to, but nobody seemed to know where you were. Anyway, I'm glad you're pleased to see me. I sort of thought maybe something was wrong. I haven't gotten any letters from you lately."

"Oh, I know. I'm sorry about that. We've been awfully busy lately."

"Too busy to write me a note once in a while?"

"Look, Mack, we really have been busy. And, I'm just not a very good letter writer. And I've never felt particularly guilty about not writing, so there it is. I am glad to see you, but I'm still half asleep, and I don't feel like arguing, and I need a cup of coffee to get my eyelids unglued, so let's go somewhere and get one, okay?"

It was not exactly the enthusiastic welcome Gerber had expected, but given the circumstance, he could understand her being a bit grouchy, so he let it slide.

Gerber glanced at his watch. "I've got a better idea. Why don't you grab a quick shower, and we'll go get something to eat. It's nearly seventeen hundred. Say, you're not late for work, are you?"

She shook her head. "No. I worked a double shift last night. I'm off till eight tomorrow morning."

"Okay. Suppose we get cleaned up, get some dinner, and go out on the town. There's got to be something to do in a town this size."

"We don't have showers in the rooms here. We've got to use the communal facilities down the hall. Why don't you go back to your room and take a shower too? I'll meet you downstairs in an hour. Did you bring any clean clothes?"

"Only jungle fatigues, I'm afraid. I didn't know Bates was going to give me the time off. Also, I haven't got a room yet. Thought I might splurge and get a hotel room downtown. That's not a problem, though. I can get a shower over at the Special Forces compound. I've got to go there to pick up my gear anyway." Gerber stood up and waited to see if she was going to offer him a kiss.

He had to settle for a smile. "Fine. See you in an hour."

Gerber made arrangements to leave his web gear and rifle at the SFOB, grabbed his pack, which contained his spare set of fatigues and some personal items, and hunted up the showers. Afterward, he judged he was early enough to drop by the PCOD lounge and have a drink before picking up Karen. As he pushed open the door of the Playboy Club, he recognized a man standing with his back against the bar, a beer clinched firmly in his fist. It was Dave Henderson.

"Hey Henderson, you're supposed to drink that thing, not squeeze it to death," Gerber called out.

"Mack Gerber! What brings you to this resort town? You still taking good care of my camp?"

"It was my camp, and it always will be my camp, you sorry individual," Gerber shouted back. "I built it, and I paid for it. I just let you house sit it for a while, while I was off doing more exciting things."

"Okay, okay, I surrender. Come on over here and have a drink. You remember my team sergeant, Jesse Bowman? This guy next to him here trying to drink all the beer in the bar is Rick Bunnell, my new XO."

Gerber nodded toward Bowman and the other man, and arched an eyebrow at Henderson. "Lieutenant Orwell?"

For just a moment, Henderson's smile vanished, and his eyes took on a thousand-yard stare. "He DEROS'ed early. In a box."

"Sorry to hear that," said Gerber, meaning it.

"Me too. He was a damned good trooper. And so young. They're all so fucking young." He grinned lopsidedly. "Except for the old geezers like you and me, and Master Sergeant Bowman, here. Ain't that right, Jesse? Hey, Jesse, how the hell old are you, anyway?"

"A hundred and seventy-two."

"See, I told you he was an old geezer like us. Bottomless Bunnell, here, on the other hand, is a mere babe in arms. You can tell he hasn't been fully weaned yet by the bottle permanently affixed to his lips." He clapped the young first lieutenant roughly on the shoulder.

Bunnell drained the beer, set the bottle down on the bar, and smilingly belched in Henderson's face. Everyone laughed, and

Bunnell went back to drinking Miller like the Russians were in Milwaukee.

"Is he always this talkative?" asked Gerber.

"No, but he's always this polite. The men call him Bush-hog because he's so suave. Actually, we just came in off a three-week patrol with an ARVN ranger company. It was a bust, of course. You can't go tromping around in the bush for three weeks with that big of a force without Charlie knowing you're coming a long time before you get there. The rangers do have better noise discipline than your average Marvin Arvin, but, well..." He let the sentence trail off. "Anyway, Bunnell ran out of beer after about the first two minutes, and he's been dying of thirst ever since."

"So, you're working with the rangers now?"

"Nah. It was just a one-shot deal. SFHQ in Saigon is putting in a new A-camp east of Dak To in the Highlands. We're gonna go in and set it up. Seems kind of like we're getting to be specialists in building camps and turning them over to somebody else. Wish the hell they'd let us settle in one spot for a while. Anyway, what'll you have to drink?"

"Beam's Choice, straight up."

Henderson ordered for Gerber, then found them a table. They sat and talked over largely unimportant matters while Bunnell kept a steadily increasing build-up of empty bottles going at the bar.

"Doesn't he ever get drunk?" Gerber asked finally.

"Sure," said Henderson, "but he's always ready to go the next day. Besides that, he's got a good rapport with the indigenous troops, and a tactical deviousness that at times scares the hell out of me. He'll make a good Special Forces man one of these days. If his liver holds out."

Gerber finally realized he'd stayed longer than he'd planned, and said a hurried goodbye to Henderson and his men. He was nearly twenty minutes late when he pulled up in front of the nurses' quarters. Karen was waiting for him outside.

She was wearing a yellow cotton dress, and she kissed him as she climbed into the jeep. "Hmmm. You've been drinking without me."

"I'll do it more often if it gets me kissed," teased Gerber. "I ran into some Special Forces types I knew over at the Playboy Club. I only had one drink, so you don't have much catching up to do. Sorry I'm late."

"Playboy Club? What's that?"

"That's what we call the PCOD lounge over at the SFOB," Gerber replied.

"All right, Mister Acronym. What's an SFOB, and while you're at it, what's a PCOD?"

"Special Forces Operating Base, our compound here. SFHQ used to be here until a couple of months ago. MACV moved command down to Saigon where they could keep a closer eye on us unconventional types. Logistics is still here, along with most of our area studies specialists and other support facilities. PCOD means personnel coming off duty. We don't have separate officer's and NCO clubs in Special Forces. We fight together, and we drink together, as a general rule. Most of the regular army types don't think much of the idea. Anyway, the local PCOD lounge is called the Playboy Club."

"Got any bunnies over there?" Morrow asked with a grin.

Gerber kept his face straight. "No bunnies. I do seem to recall having seen a stuffed tiger's head, once."

"Yuck. Sounds barbaric."

"It's better than a stuffed bunny," Gerber retorted. "Well, it may not be better, but it's less barbaric. Depends on what you stuff the bunny with."

Morrow made a face at him, grinning and biting her lower lip.

"So where do you want to eat?" asked Gerber.

"That comes later," she said saucily. "First you've got to buy me supper."

"Okay. Fine," laughed Gerber. "Just tell me where to, ma'am, and I'll be happy to drive you there."

"There's a place about ten kilometers down the highway called Francois's. They serve huge lobster and crayfish. Do you know it?"

"Never ate there, but I think I can find it." Gerber put the jeep in gear and they drove off.

They had gone only a few miles down Highway 1 when they passed a dense stand of sugarcane on their right, in the direction of the rail line. Gerber noted that it looked like a good spot for an ambush, and silently wished he'd brought his rifle, as they would be returning after dark. Almost instantly, he chided himself for being paranoid. There was seldom much enemy activity this close to Nha Trang. The area was fairly pacified, and besides, Charlie needed his recreational opportunities too. So the Viet Cong tended to leave the immediate area of Nha Trang pretty much alone, and concentrated their activities in the smaller villages in the surrounding countryside. Still, there was Kepler's warning about the new VC terrorist campaign targeting Special Forces personnel. Gerber decided he was glad he'd worn his .45 pistol.

Upon their arrival at Francois's, Gerber realized he didn't have to worry about being underdressed. True, most of the other Americans in evidence were clothed in khakis or civilian garb, but the owner had been in business there for some time, and had long ago grown used to having Special Forces men from their big camp in nearby Nha Trang as his patrons. He had become accustomed to their tendency toward a more casual style of dress. Besides, Special Forces were among his oldest customers, and, on average, he'd found them to be more generous tippers than the new batch of Americans who had followed them in and enlarged the base.

They ordered champagne cocktails, because it seemed like the thing to do, and Gerber opted for the crayfish, having already eaten lobster once within the last week.

"Can you recommend a good white wine?" Morrow asked the waiter.

"Of course, mademoiselle. We have an excellent selection of Beaujolais and Chablis."

It was one of those things that never ceased to amaze Gerber about Vietnam. War and poverty could be raging in the countryside, yet in the larger towns you could still get a four-star meal and a bottle of good French wine to go with it.

The waiter seemed to hesitate. "But perhaps mademoiselle et monsieur desire something *special supplementaire*?"

Gerber wasn't sure he liked the way the man mixed his languages. "Just how extra special is it?" he asked.

"It is regrettably expensive, monsieur, but I am very pleased to be able to tell you that we have just come into possession of a single case of very fine white burgundy, Pouilly-Fuissé 1959. It was a very good year for the Chardonnay, and is a much better wine than we are accustomed to having here."

"And just how regrettably expensive a year was it for the Chardonnay?" Gerber asked.

"Eighteen hundred piastres."

Gerber flipped the figure over in his head. It was more than the price of the meal, and in fact, represented a good chunk of a day's pay, but it was still less than he might have expected to pay for such a wine back in The World.

"What do you think?" Morrow asked him, leaning forward.

"I think," said Gerber, "that it would be a well-balanced light-bodied wine, dry and a bit fruity with a delicate green-gold color."

"Ah, monsieur, you know the wine. Truly you have touched my heart," said the waiter.

"And truly, you have touched my pocketbook. Lightly chilled, if you please."

"But of course."

"So now you're a wine expert," said Morrow, when the waiter had withdrawn.

Gerber shrugged. "A Special Forces officer has to be well rounded in all areas of his education. Besides, when you're a captain, you have to know these things."

Morrow studied him for a moment, a sly smile spreading slowly across her lips. "Well, Mr. Know-it-all, I'll bet I know something that you don't."

"Okay," said Gerber, "I'll go along with the gag. What is it?"

She leaned forward, winked, and gave him that funny grin, biting her lower lip. "I'm not wearing any underpants."

Gerber was simultaneously shocked and fascinated. "Really?"

"Really. And you know what else? I'm not wearing a bra, either. In fact, you might say I'm naked under my clothes."

"You know," said Gerber, "I don't think I've ever had dinner before with a lady who was naked under her clothes."

"Then it's a virgin experience for you, is it?" she laughed. "Well, what I want to know is, what are you going to do about it?"

"I'm going to try very hard not to think about it, until I've finished my dinner," said Gerber.

"And after dinner?"

"Then I'm going to try very hard to think about it. A lot."

The next morning, Gerber planned an early exit from the nurses' quarters in order to avoid being seen coming out of Morrow's room. Although he was spied by a couple of nurses down the hallway, they took no particular interest in him, other than mildly curious glances, and the sleep-eyed clerk at the sign-in desk paid him no attention at all.

He went first to the SFOB to pick up his gear, and to get a shave and a shower, although he had to put the same clothes back on. Then he drove downtown and dropped his other uniform off at a local laundry that offered same-day service. After that, he went hotel hunting.

After a couple of hours of checking out possibilities, he found a room at the Regence. The hotel had been built during the French occupation of Indochina, and was still owned and managed by a Frenchman who had stayed on after the withdrawal. As such, it was better furnished and better maintained than most. The room was huge, well-appointed in the old French colonial style, with a huge brass-fitted bed, and, wonder of wonders, a bathtub. The water from the tap was rusty for only the first few seconds, and the hot water was actually hot. The hotel was a reasonable distance from the beach, and only slightly outrageously overpriced. Gerber took the room for two nights.

Afterward, realizing he hadn't eaten, he had a late breakfast at a sidewalk cafe a couple of blocks from the hotel, and then went out to buy a pair of swimming trunks. That turned out to be a difficult task because he didn't know how to say swimming trunks in Vietnamese. He finally managed to convey the general idea to a French-speaking shop owner.

Equipped with the new trunks, Gerber armed himself with half a dozen beers and a .50-caliber ammo can filled with ice, and set off for the beach.

It was a beautiful day, the sky clear and bright, and it felt good to lie in the warm, white sand and listen to the surf and watch the seabirds hunting fish, and the shore birds searching for clams along the water's edge.

He and Karen had made love along that same stretch of beach last night, first in a quiet fury of passion, like two animals trying to devour one another, then later, after a swim, slowly and tenderly, with the star-studded Southeast Asian sky overhead, and their bodies stretched out along each other in the moonlight.

There had been no noisy soldiers playing volleyball and shouting obscenities to each other in the sand, no helicopters chattering overhead, carrying troops into the field or carrying wounded to the hospital. The war had seemed so very far away then. Today it seemed much closer, but the beach and the beer, the sun and the birds, and the incredibly blue sky all gave it a kind of unreal quality, like sitting too close to the screen at a drive-in movie. Gerber knew what the helicopters meant, but they didn't affect him directly. He could ignore them if he so chose. It wasn't a perfect day, but it was still a good one.

A little after three, he decided to call it an afternoon. The last of the beer was gone, and the suntan lotion was running low. Despite almost six months in Vietnam, he still had a tendency to sunburn his legs.

He picked up his uniform from the laundry, and was mildly irritated to see the knife-edged crease that had been pressed into the pants. Tomorrow he'd have to remember to tell them no starch. Then he went back to his hotel room and regretfully took a quick bath, promising himself a long soak later, and got dressed.

Morrow was late getting off work, and arrived just as Gerber was inquiring about her at the desk. Her hair was disheveled, her fatigues were bloodstained, and there was a vacant, tired look in her eyes. She walked up to Gerber, but stared past him, as though looking at something over his left shoulder.

"Take me out of here," she said. "I need a drink. I need a lot of drinks."

"Of course," said Gerber. "I think maybe you ought to go up and change first. You've, ah, got something on your uniform."

She looked down, as if noticing the blood for the first time, and seemed surprised to find it there. Nodding mutely, she turned and trudged up the stairs. Gerber followed.

In her room, she stripped off her clothes, letting them fall into a pile. She didn't even bother to kick them away.

"Wait here," she said, picking up a towel. "Please."

"Sure." Gerber nodded and sat down on the edge of her bunk.

She was gone a long time, and when she finally returned, dripping wet from her shower, she looked even more tired than before.

"Look, we don't have to go anyplace tonight, if you don't want to," Gerber offered.

Morrow sank down on the folding steel chair and looked at him. She even managed a weak smile. "Thanks for the offer. It's okay. I just want you to understand that I may not be too much fun tonight. Okay?"

"Understood."

"Okay. Then do me a favor, will you? Before I get dressed, come over here and give me a hug. I really need a hug right now."

Gerber walked over and took her in his arms. He held her for what must have been five minutes, neither of them speaking. Finally she pushed him away.

"Thanks. That was nice. Any more though, and I might fall asleep. Let's go over to the Club Nautique and get something to eat." She rummaged in the tiny closet, pulled out a clean set of fatigues, then held them out at arm's length, looked at them, and sighed. "I hope you don't mind, especially after you took the trouble to get your uniform pressed, you look really nice tonight, but I just don't feel much like a dress this evening."

"I understand. What do you want to do first, dinner or a drink?"

"Drink, I think," she said, pulling on the fatigues. "Maybe a couple. Then dinner. After that we'll see."

They went over to the New York Bar, found a table, and Gerber ordered them both a double shot of Beam's. Morrow drank hers in one gulp, and Gerber ordered her another. She drank it in two gulps, and motioned for a third.

"Okay," she said, "I'll slow down now."

Gerber nodded slightly. "I take it today was a bad day at the hospital."

Morrow gave a sardonic chuckle. "They're all bad days. Today was really rotten."

"Want to talk about it?" Gerber asked carefully.

"No. Yes. I don't know. What good would it do? What good does any of it do?"

"Look, I'm sorry. If you want answers, talk to the chaplain. Half the time, I don't even know what the questions are. If you want to talk, I'll listen. If you don't want to talk, fine. I was just trying to be helpful. Sometimes it helps to talk about things."

Morrow took a sip from her glass. Her hand trembled slightly. "Told you I wouldn't be very good company." She seemed almost defiant.

"That's fine. You're not required to be. I just made you an offer. You're free to refuse it."

She was quiet for a moment, and Gerber thought perhaps she'd decided to do exactly that, then she spoke.

"The Viet Cong ambushed a big ARVN patrol out toward Plei Me this morning, just about dawn. One American advisor was killed, and three others wounded. I don't know how many ARVN were killed, and I don't much care. They called out helicopter gunships to support them, and the Viet Cong shot down some of the gunships. And then they called out the medevacs and the Viet Cong shot down some of those too. We had dead and wounded Americans coming in every half hour or so until two o'clock this afternoon.

"You people go out and make the war, but we see the results of it," Morrow continued. "We see the traumatic amputees and the double amputees, and the paraplegics and the quads. We see the sucking chest wounds, and the guys who come in here trying to hold their own intestines inside after they've had their abdomens ripped open. We see the guys with no fingers, or no hands, or with their eyes put out. Sometimes they haven't even got a face. Sometimes they're burned from white phosphorus or napalm that got dropped too close. Sometimes they're so riddled with shrapnel that we can't even get it all out. We just dig out the bigger pieces and leave the little ones inside. Then we patch them up as best we can, and some major or colonel comes in and pins a Purple Heart onto their pillowcase, and we send whatever pieces are left of them home to their families and girlfriends. Sometimes there aren't even pieces to send home.

"One of the guys they brought in this morning was a young helicopter pilot. He got trapped in his aircraft when it was shot down trying to medevac some wounded, and he had burns over ninety to a hundred percent of his body. I was working in triage when he came in about ten this morning, and his hands were burned so bad I was going to cut his gloves off, and then I realized he wasn't wearing any gloves. He died about three-thirty this afternoon. He was a nineteen-year-old kid from the medevac unit here, and I knew him. And when they brought him in this morning, he was burned so bad that I didn't even recognize him."

Her voice broke and she buried her face in her hands. "Oh, Jesus, I was there when he died, and he was such a mess the medics wouldn't touch him. I had to put him in the bag myself."

Gerber wanted to tell her that he understood. That he'd seen all those things, or most of them, anyway, and that he knew what it meant to lose someone you knew, someone you were close to, which was why you learned to make buddies with everyone and friends with no one. Because a buddy could save your life, but a friend hurt too much when he died. So after it had happened a few times, you promised yourself you'd never let yourself get that close to someone again. Yet he knew it wasn't the same thing. He at least saw people killed in battle. He at least could feel rage, and strike back. Sometimes futilely, it was true, but also sometimes with satisfaction. She saw only the aftermath, could only watch young men maimed and dying.

Gerber knew that at a time like this, anything he could say would sound hollow and false, no matter how true it might be.

He did the only thing he could think of to do. He got slowly up from his chair and stepped to her, and took her in his arms.

She tried to shake him off, but he held her tightly.

"It's all right," he whispered. "It's all right to cry."

And then she did.

After a while, he took her out to the jeep, because people in the bar were staring at them. It had made him feel angry, and Gerber had wanted to shout at them. To say, "What's the matter with you assholes, haven't you ever seen anybody feel before? Haven't you ever seen anybody care?" But he'd said nothing. Instead, he'd led her out to the jeep, and helped her in, and sat with her while she cried, and cried with her, sharing her grief. Morrow cried for all the hurt she'd seen, for all the hurt she'd felt for others, and Gerber cried with her because he understood, and cared about her, and wanted to share her hurt. It was the first time he'd cried since Korea, and that had been the first time he'd cried since he was twelve.

When they'd both used up all their tears, he asked softly, "Karen, do you want me to take you back to your room?"

She took the handkerchief he offered, and wiped at her dry, swollen, red eyes.

"No," she said, after a time. "I don't want to be alone."

So he drove them back to the Regence, and took her up to his room, and they got into bed and held each other. And after a long time, finally, they slept.

CHAPTER 7

THE JUNGLE NEAR AHN TAP

Truc Nguyen Bong and five of his companions stood at a semblance of attention before the rickety table in the small thatched hootch, their body positions contorted because their elbows had been lashed tightly together behind their backs. A kerosene lamp flickered sporadically upon the otherwise bare surface of the table, and seated behind it in a folding metal chair was Major Huynh Dong Long, commanding officer of the 129th Main Force VC Battalion. Slightly to his left stood an advisor from the People's Liberation Army of Communist China, his face obscured by shadows.

Major Huynh had once commanded the 123rd Main Force VC Battalion, which had been destroyed nearly half a year ago in an unsuccessful attempt to overrun the nearby Special Forces camp and drive the American and South Vietnamese soldiers from the region. Huynh had taken three companies of Main Force VC and nearly one hundred local guerrillas into that battle, and had come out of it with less than a platoon. The Americans with their Tai mercenaries and South Vietnamese allies had not only devastated his command, they had broken the back of the supporting Main Force AWF Regiment. Sometime later, the remnants of the Viet Cong forces had been reorganized into the 129th Main Force Battalion, and Huynh, as senior surviving officer, had been given command. Huynh had once been famed for his fine sense of humor, even in the darkest situations. It was said, however, that he had lost more than the men under his command in that battle. Since that time, no one could recall having seen him smile. Tonight, as he faced the six prisoners in front of him, his face was an implacable mask.

Huynh eyed the men briefly, gave a disgusted snort, and spoke. "Comrade Truc, you and your subordinate agents stand accused of treason to the people's revolutionary movement, the NLF, and the Viet Cong San. Further, you are accused of exceeding your authority, acting without proper authorization, and placing personal considerations above those of the People's Revolutionary Reunification Movement. Have you anything to say in your defense before judgment is passed?"

"Comrade Major," Truc spoke with trembling lips, "I have no knowledge of these serious criticisms of my behavior. On what are they based?"

"The specifications of the charges are that fifteen nights ago, you and your subordinate agents from the Ahn Taps carried out the execution of the schoolteacher and one of the shopkeepers from the village of Anh Tap, that you did so without the prior knowledge and approval of higher authority, and that your action caused serious damage to the revolutionary liberation effort. Do you deny this?"

"Comrade Major, I do not. The woman was a propaganda agent of the imperialist Americans and their Saigon puppet government. She was teaching counterrevolutionary politics in her classes that threatened to sway the villagers away from our cause. The man was known to be sympathetic to the Saigon government, and had been openly critical of the people's struggle for liberation on a number of previous occasions. Their executions were carried out in the approved manner for dealing with collaborators of the Saigon puppets. I freely admit my shortcomings in not first seeking the approval of my superiors in carrying out the executions, but the situation demanded immediate action, and I was unable to delay until the proper approval could be obtained. I acted in good faith and out of genuine concern for the safety of the revolutionary movement. My subordinates also acted in good faith upon my instructions. We eliminated a serious threat to the stability of revolutionary thought in the village by the elimination of these traitors to the revolutionary liberation reunification movement. We caused no harm to the revolutionary effort and committed no treason."

Truc felt he was on solid ground here. He couldn't understand why they were being treated as criminals instead of heroes. Had they not sacrificed the comfortable life they had established for themselves in the village in order to further the aims of the revolutionary movement by removing two enemies of the war of liberation? Those two had been spreading lies about the goals of the communist party, which was to reunify Vietnam.

"Do you deny that you courted this woman, and that she rejected your advances?"

"Comrade Major, I do not. I merely submit that it had no bearing on my actions or those of my subordinates. We eliminated two enemies of the revolution. I repeat that we committed no treason."

"Comrade Truc, one of our agents in Ahn Tap who is unknown to you has reported that the very action for which you seem to feel you should be praised has succeeded in driving the villagers into the hands of the enemy. They were merely angered by the death of this schoolteacher who was of no importance to us. But they were outraged by the death of the shopkeeper Ngoc who was well-known and respected in the community, and by the nature of the unjustifiable mutilations which bespoke a personal vendetta on your part.

The villagers have denounced all known Viet Cong agents and sympathizers to the Americans, and provided them with information that enabled the imperialists to damage or destroy over seven tons of supplies critical to our upcoming offensive, and to kill or wound twenty-seven of our soldiers. If this is not treason, it is, at the very least, criminal stupidity. Such incompetence cannot be tolerated in the people's struggle for liberation. Your subordinates are no less responsible for complying with your stupidity without questioning or criticizing it."

Huynh had spoken in a cold, emotionless tone that was almost a whisper. Now he raised his voice slightly, so that it approached a normal level, but it remained flat and utterly devoid of feeling.

"Comrade Truc, the evidence against you and your subordinates is clear. Due to the exigencies of war, your right to a trial in a People's Court is suspended. The sentence is death. The executions to be carried out immediately."

He turned to the commander of the guard detail. "Comrade Sergeant, take these men out and shoot them."

The prisoners were marched out the door.

"Rather a harsh punishment for merely being stupid, don't you think, Comrade?"

Huynh turned sharply in his chair. The face of the Chinese advisor was still cast in shadow, but a faintly glowing cigarette marked the approximate location of his mouth.

"These are harsh times," answered Huynh. "Would you have me show leniency toward men who have cost us the lives of two dozen troops, who have destroyed irreplaceable supplies needed for the revolutionary effort, and turned a village of nearly fifteen hundred peasants against us? These men cost us the loss of fourteen sampans that in the future could have transported hundreds, perhaps thousands, of tons of arms and materials. An example must be made."

"Yes, Comrade, I agree. An example must be made. But is it wise to make this particular example? Would it not be better to shoot only this incompetent Truc fellow, and let the others live, so that they might learn from his example?"

For the first time, Huynh showed emotion in his voice, something akin to anger. "Are you questioning my authority to have these men shot, Comrade Advisor?"

"Neither your authority, nor your right, Major. Merely your wisdom. Is it not counterproductive to kill so many of our own men unnecessarily?"

"Was it counterproductive for them to turn an entire village against us by the execution of two collaborators with the enemy?"

"I do not disagree that their actions were a mistake in this instance, nor that the men were negligent in not seeking the approval of higher authority for the executions to be carried out. But such a program of political assassination is established policy for dealing with sympathizers of the Saigon junta. I myself would have approved of the executions, although perhaps not of the finishing touches."

Outside, there was a rifle shot, followed after a moment by another, and then slowly by four more, making the advisor's objections academic.

"So you yourself would have approved of the executions, would you, Comrade?" asked Huynh softly.

"Yes. I would have."

"Then, Comrade, you would have been a fool. I sometimes wonder whether or not you Chinese will ever understand us. We are grateful for the arms you supply to our struggle, and to the excellent training you provide. Your knowledge in particular, Comrade, of the nature of the tactics employed by the Americans, is invaluable. But while you are a military genius, you are politically naive. You do not grasp that ours is not merely a war of liberation, but truly a civil war.

"I have two brothers," continued Huynh. "One of them is a farmer in the north, near Hanoi. The other is a secret policeman in Saigon. You Chinese do not understand either the nature of our struggle, nor the nature of our people. You forget, Comrade, that I myself was born in the Ahn Taps. I lived there until I was twelve years old. I could have told you what the reaction of the villagers would have been to the assassination of Ong Ngoc Diem Bai. He was my uncle."

The Chinese advisor was silent for a long time. At last he took a final puff on his cigarette, and stubbed it out on the top of the unsteady table. Then he carefully stripped the paper from the butt and scattered the remaining tobacco before rolling the paper into a tiny ball which he ground into the dirt floor of the hootch with his boot heel. At last he spoke.

"Then Comrade, you are faced with a truly difficult decision."

"The village?"

"Yes. What will you do?"

Huynh sighed deeply. "I will do what must be done. Those young fools I have just executed destroyed in a single night the trust and tolerance that it took many years to build. What has been damaged so, cannot be repaired. I fear that I must set one more example, lest the other villages learn the wrong lesson from Ahn Tap."

"When will you do it?"

"Tomorrow night. Before I have time to think about what must be done, and lose the nerve to do it. I will take my soldiers into the village of Ahn Tap, and I will destroy it."

CHAPTER 8

SPECIAL FORCES CAMP A-555

Bromhead was sitting in Gerber's office, swearing softly to himself as he tried to figure out the jigsaw-puzzle forms necessary to requisition an additional supply of toilet paper for the latrines. He supposed Sergeant Fetterman would have known how to do it properly in fifteen seconds flat, but the wiry master sergeant was still trying to get the motorboat operating properly, and the young lieutenant was reluctant to bother him, since Fetterman seemed to be the only one in the whole camp who knew anything about outboard marine engines.

Fetterman had been busy ten and fifteen hours a day since the river ambush of the VC sampan convoy, working to repair the little craft and improve its armament. The holes in the fiberglass hull had been caulked with tar, covered over with tin plates bolted through the hull, sealed, and painted. A fiberglass auto body patch-up kit would have made the job simple. Without a convenient neighborhood K-Mart located in the jungle, the task had taken two days. Then the engine had to be overhauled. Two spark plug wires were replaced with spares intended for the camp's two jeeps. They didn't fit properly and had to be modified. The spark plugs were fouled and had to be cleaned with JP-4 from the small fuel-storage tank at the end of the runway. One of them had been shattered by a bullet, leaving only five spares. Bromhead had written his parents, asking them to try and find the appropriate plugs and mail him a dozen, along with a couple of sets of points. Those in the engine had been burned, but Fetterman had made them operable by carefully cleaning them with a fine grit sanding paper. Fortunately, the tool kit in the boat had included a set of gap gauges, but there had been no manual, and Fetterman had been forced to experiment by trial and error. Then there had been the problem of refueling the little boat. Although there was an ample supply of gasoline available at the camp, it needed to be mixed with oil to be usable in the two-cycle outboard. Since there had been no outboard oil available, Fetterman had suggested mixing the gas with SAE 30 weight motor oil in a ratio of fifty to one. The engine digested the mix all right, but it did seem to make the plugs more prone to fouling, so they required frequent cleaning.

Today, Fetterman and Tyme had spent the morning installing a protective barrier of quarter-inch steel plate around the engine housing to protect it from small arms fire. It wouldn't stop a direct hit, but it might turn a grazing round. The problem there, of course, was that it put extra weight on the transom, and tended to make the engine overheat, especially if it was operated during the afternoon, when the day was at its hottest.

During the afternoon, the two men had installed a new twin gun mount, replacing the single mount between the seats, so that the motorboat now mounted three .30-cal. machine guns. The 40mm grenade launcher had been retained to provide the boat with some indirect fire capability, but had been relocated to the driver's position, as had the radio. The fourth crewman would now become strictly a gunner, using a 3.5-inch rocket launcher to give the miniature gunboat more punch.

The task of fixing up the boat had been complicated by the necessity of removing it from the camp to avoid its discovery. Bromhead had no idea who was looking for it, but Gerber's message had made it clear enough that somebody important in Saigon was hunting it, somebody with enough clout to drop in on them by air, unannounced. Bromhead was slightly relieved that no such visit had yet occurred. That could mean whoever wanted their boat back had lost the trail and wouldn't be coming after all, or it could mean they were waiting until they were sure of their facts before lowering the boom. In any event, they wouldn't have an easy time finding the boat even if they did trace it to the camp. It was now tied up at a new dock in a small cut on the river below the camp, thoroughly camouflaged, and guarded by two squads of Lieutenant Bao's best Tai strikers, under the command of Sergeant Krung. The original dock, near the bridge north of the camp, had been dismantled, and the boat ramp had been improved and camouflaged so that it was not obvious except to someone who knew exactly where to look for it. The trailer had been hidden by the simple method of submerging it under the water on the ramp, and anchoring it to stakes driven into the river bottom so that it wouldn't drift away.

Now, as dusk approached, all was in readiness. If Fetterman's final adjustments proved out on the engine, Bromhead intended to let him take the boat out after dark and patrol the river south and east of the camp, toward the Ahn Taps. The reports from the village chief there of continuing low-key Viet Cong activity led Bromhead to believe it might prove a profitable patrol area. This plan had the distinct advantage of not reusing the sandspit ambush position, which the VC had become familiar with.

Bromhead belatedly realized that, while he had been preoccupied with thoughts of Fetterman and the boat, he had written rocket launcher in the tiny space where he should have penned toilet paper. He inked out the error, and then discovered that there wasn't enough space left for the correct words. Disgustedly, he crumpled the form into a ball and tossed it in the general direction of the wastebasket. The shot missed.

"Looks like your aim is off a little bit today, Lieutenant. You might try dribbling before you shoot. Get your timing down better that way." It was Fetterman.

"Good evening, Master Sergeant. How's the boat shaping up?"

"Humming like a sewing machine, sir. It does miss a stitch now and then, but it's as good as I can make it. Armament's ready and the ammo's on board. We going to take her out this evening?"

"Yes, but you know the policy about leaving the camp without an American officer. I'm afraid the honor is going to be all yours."

Fetterman made no false pretense at hiding his glee. "Great, sir. Would it be okay if I take Sergeant McMillan with me? He's been helping fix up the boat. Says he's getting sick of sticking Band Aids on cuts and lancing boils."

"I suppose the Doc is entitled to some patrol duty. If he wants to stay up all night and maybe get shot at, I guess that's okay with me. Might not be a bad idea to have a medic along. You guys will be operating pretty far from camp tonight."

"It's only about ten klicks, sir."

"Which is a long way to carry a wounded man if your engine conks out again. Tell Doc I said he can go."

"Thank you sir. Boom-Boom too?"

"Yes, Boom-Boom too. Provided Sergeant Tyme's got his life insurance paid up. Seems like every time the Captain or I let you two go out together, you stir the shit with a big stick. Who you got in mind for the fourth member of your crew?"

"Hadn't decided yet. I suppose I'd better take one of the RFs. After all, it is their war. It'll have to be somebody who's handy with a three-five or a thirty. I'll ask Minh to recommend someone."

"Fine. Take anybody you want, just so long as Lieutenant Minh gives his approval."

"Delighted to hear you say that, old boy," said Minh, sticking his head through the doorway, "because I've got just the chap for you. Me."

"You?"

"Yes, quite. Providing Master Sergeant Fetterman here has no serious objection to having me in his crew. This water-mobile concept fascinates me. We have so many rivers and canals in my country, don't you know. Well, I haven't had any opportunity to observe one of your little river ambushes, and now that you have this new boat of yours, I'm twice as keen to see one. Besides, I am rather handy with either a rocket launcher or a Browning. The bayonet isn't my only strong point."

Bromhead looked noticeably uncomfortable. Lieutenant Minh had been the senior member of the LLDB A-team since the death of Captain Trang. Although Minh would normally have been Bromhead's counterpart, Trang had not been replaced, and Minh had been appointed acting camp commander. As such, he was now Gerber's counterpart, and technically speaking, ran the show, since the role of the American Special Forces personnel was an advisory one. Camp A-555 tended to function more on the order of an equal partnership, however, a situation with which both Minh and the Americans were well satisfied, although it did not conform to the official policy established by the Saigon command.

Bromhead had no misgivings about Minh's ability. He had had a chance to work closely with the Vietnamese officer on a number of combat missions and knew him to be an outstanding soldier and leader. His clipped English accent, the product of an expensive foreign education that had included the British Military Academy at Sandhurst, could be a bit unsettling at times, but the man was a hard charger, and a thorough professional. Unlike many of his countrymen, he was not the least bit afraid of a fight, and had already distinguished himself with considerable valor under fire.

What concerned Bromhead was that allowing Minh to accompany Fetterman would leave the camp with no Vietnamese officer. Lieutenant Bao, who commanded the two Tai strike companies, although a South Vietnamese citizen, was himself, like his men, an ethnic Tai, and there was a good deal of prejudice between most of the Tais and Vietnamese. Bromhead couldn't be certain that the Vietnamese troops who made up the rest of the camp's complement of men would obey an order from Bao, or from himself. He felt reasonably comfortable with the rest of the LLDB, including the new Vietnamese team sergeant, Thuong Si Hoai, and the senior sergeant in nominal charge of the Regional Forces strike companies, Trung Si Nhat Pham, but he couldn't be sure of the RFs themselves. They had on occasion proved to be less than completely reliable.

The problem left Bromhead with a thorny dilemma. On the one hand, he could not refuse Minh permission to go. As camp commander, Minh could pretty much do whatever he wanted. On the other hand, he didn't want to get caught short in a crunch. He conveyed his misgivings to Minh in as diplomatic a manner as possible, and advised against his accompanying the patrol.

"Thanks old chap, for not refusing," said Minh, when Bromhead had finished. "I choose to ignore your advice, and am informing you of same in front of the Master Sergeant here as witness, which lets you off the hook. If anything goes wrong, I'll be the one with the blotted copybook. Now then, let's ask Master Sergeant Fetterman if he objects to having me in his crew."

Fetterman looked at Bromhead, who shrugged. "Like you said, Tony, it is his war."

"In that case, sir, I'd be delighted to have Lieutenant Minh in company." Fetterman turned toward the Vietnamese officer. "Which station will you prefer Trung Uy, the twin .30 cal. or the rocket launcher?"

"The launcher, I think, if there is no objection from Sergeant Tyme. I've always been an advocate of the one shot, one hit philosophy, and you can hit so much harder with a rocket launcher. Besides," he smiled, "the white phosphorus makes such lovely patterns. Don't you agree?"

"Fine sir. Please be at the south gate at twenty hundred hours with whatever personal gear you might wish to bring. Do you have a flak jacket, sir?"

"Yes," answered Minh, "but I seldom wear it on patrol. It's a bit heavy and tends to slow me down. Your American vests aren't really built for the Asian frame, either."

"Please wear it, sir. Uniform of the day is helmets and flak jackets for all the crew. We're just too damned exposed in the boat."

"Hmmm. Yes, I can see your point, Sergeant. It's not practical to armor the boat, so we must armor the crew. I'll do as you ask. Now, if you gentlemen will excuse me, I want to grab supper before I check our perimeter. It's nearly time to stand to."

Shortly after 2000 hours Fetterman, Tyme, McMillan, and Minh filed out the south gate of the camp and down the path through the minefield to the outer wire. Once clear of the perimeter, they made their way across the open killing ground that extended for another three hundred meters beyond the wire, then moved along a rice paddy dike that cut through a marshy area, and slipped into the narrow band of jungle that paralleled the river. As they approached the tiny cove where the motorboat was sheltered, they were challenged by Sergeant Krung's sentries, who were expecting them, and passed on through. After loading aboard personal gear and making a final weapons check and fuel inventory, they weighed anchor and set out for the Ahn Taps. The time was 2045 hours.

The evening was clear for a change, the moon was bright, illuminating the water, although the banks of the river remained in shadow. Fetterman ran the little craft up to twenty mph, standing up in order to be better able to see any snags or sandbars. Doc McMillan, half kneeling on the foredeck behind the bow .30 cal., also kept a sharp eye out for submerged objects. Tyme continually swept the riverbanks from behind the twin .30-cal. mount, ready to instantly return suppressive fire in the event of an ambush. Minh, in the rear, did likewise, a white phosphorus rocket for the bazooka held ready between his knees, Fetterman's M-79 resting loaded in the crook of one arm. This was the weapon with which they would respond first in the event they were ambushed, because of its capability of delivering immediate suppression on target. The arrangement left Fetterman free to maneuver the boat, while giving Minh a choice of weapons. If the Green Berets and their LLDB companion sighted enemy shipping, Minh would return the grenade launcher to Fetterman and concentrate his efforts on hitting the Viet Cong boats with the rocket launcher, which had proved so devastatingly effective.

Their plan for interdicting VC vessels was to throttle back as they approached Ahn Tap 2, the largest of the three hamlets and the one which fronted directly upon the river. They would then attempt to drift past without attracting the attention of any Viet Cong observers who might be in the village, and establish an ambush at anchor in the shadows along the opposite bank downstream from the village dock. It was a simple plan, which might well have proved effective, but it never got put into operation.

When the patrol boat was still nearly three-quarters of a mile from Ahn Tap, very heavy firing erupted from the village. Fetterman quickly put the motorboat into the shallows along the opposite bank, and radioed Bromhead that a major firefight was in progress in or near Ahn Tap. He gave his position, and requested further instructions.

"Zulu Afloat, this is Five," Bromhead answered. "I have negative information of any friendly ops in the area. Stand by at your location while I check with Crystal Ball."

Perhaps fifteen minutes passed while the men in the boat waited tensely, listening to the sounds of gunfire ahead. The fighting was now punctuated at intervals by the sound of grenades and an occasional louder explosion, which Fetterman took to be either satchel charges or rocket-propelled grenades. Through the general din, the ragged hammering of a 12.7mm Degtyarev-Shpagin could be heard. At last Bromhead's voice came over the radio again.

"Zulu Afloat, this is Zulu Ops. Crystal Ball has no report of friendlies in the area. They request you investigate. Use extreme caution."

"Rog, Zulu Ops. Will investigate the situation." Fetterman put down the handset of the PRC-10. "Okay everybody, let's stay real sharp on this one. Bromhead says B-team wants us to go into the Ahn Taps and have a look-see. We'll hang along this side of the river, move down slow with the engine idling until we either encounter hostile forces or reach the dock. If we make it as far as the dock without being fired on, Boom-Boom and I will sneak ashore and have a look around. If somebody starts shooting, we'll shoot back and get the hell out in a hurry. Any questions?"

"Just one, old boy," said Minh. "Since it seems probable that we can expect a warm reception, don't you think it would be a good idea if I were to go ahead and load up the rocket launcher?"

"I think it would be mandatory," answered Fetterman. "I'll take the M-seventy-nine."

Weapons manned and ready, they crept down the shadowed bank beneath overhanging branches and vines.

Fetterman found the boat difficult to control in the shallows with only the current to drive them, and was forced to engage the prop, and increase the engine rpm slightly in order to keep the plugs from fouling. As they rounded a slight bend in the river's pathway, they could see the village ahead of them in the distance. There were tracers and RPGs pouring into the village from two sides, and a solid wall of flame along the third.

The men were painfully aware of their exposed position in the river. Still, Fetterman edged the boat forward at a snail's pace. He picked up the handset of the radio long enough to give Bromhead a quick advisory.

"Zulu Operations, this is Zulu Afloat."

Bromhead answered immediately. "This is Ops. Go."

"The village is definitely under attack," Fetterman told him. "They're taking heavy automatic weapons fire and rocket grenades. It looks like the whole village is on fire."

"Can you see the enemy?"

"Negative. Only their firing. Do you want us to try to get closer?"

"Negative," came Bromhead's firm reply. "If possible, locate and observe the enemy, but do not engage. I'll get back to you."

Bromhead contacted B-team headquarters in Saigon as soon as he finished speaking with Fetterman, and was surprised when Lieutenant Colonel Bates personally answered him.

"This is Crystal Ball Six."

"Crystal Ball, the village of Ahn Tap is under sustained ground attack. We have an observer team in the area. They report heavy automatic weapons fire and RPGs. The village is burning."

"Understood, Zulu Ops. What are your intentions?"

"Crystal Ball, I'd like to put a reaction force in there and see if we can make contact with the enemy. Also, it looks like those villagers are going to be needing beaucoup medical assistance. We do not have transport available, however, and the distance is about ten klicks. Can you arrange airlift?"

"Roger, Zulu Ops. Crystal Ball out."

Twenty-five minutes later, Bocker informed Bromhead that the first of three flights of seven helicopters each was inbound for the camp. They had had trouble scraping up aircraft at the last minute, so that was why the numbers were so strange. He also informed him that Gerber was aboard the flight lead.

Bromhead was both pleased and surprised at the news. The last he had heard, Gerber was still in Nha Trang. "Where's Schmidt?" he asked Bocker.

"Right here, Lieutenant," said the junior commo specialist, materializing from the shadows at Bromhead's shoulder.

"Christ Schmidt," Bromhead started. "Can't you announce yourself? You might give a guy a heart attack. Especially dressed like that. And take off those damned sunglasses for Christ's sake."

Schmidt was attired in his usual Count Dracula costume, M-60 slung over his right shoulder, the shoulder straps of a PRC-10 draped nonchalantly over his left.

"With respect, Lieutenant, I'd like to keep the glasses on for the time being. Don't want to ruin my visual purple. I'll take them off before we go in on the assault."

"Okay, Visual Purple. Just be sure you do. Stick close to me with that radio." He turned to Bao. "Lieutenant Bao, are your men ready to go?"

"Yes Lieutenant Johnny. We all ready. I leave Lieutenant Hung in command of other men. We go kill communists now, yes?"

"We go kill communists now," agreed Bromhead. "Where's Krung?"

Bao grinned, showing uneven teeth. "Him in charge of detail guarding boat dock tonight, remember. Him be much pissed-off when him find out we go kill communists without him."

Bromhead grinned back. Sergeant Krung's hatred of the Viet Cong was legendary among the men of Camp A-555. Several years earlier, some Viet Minh soldiers had killed his family and raped his younger sister. Krung had sworn a blood oath to kill ten communists for each member of his family after that. He kept score on a board in his hootch with the genitals of those he'd killed. "Yes, I imagine he will be a bit P-O'ed at that. Come on. Let's go meet the Captain."

As soon as the Huey-slick touched down on the runway, Gerber leaped out, spotted Bromhead, and waved him over. While the first group of Tais climbed aboard the helicopters, Gerber held a hurried conference with Bromhead.

"Good to have you back, sir. How was Nha Trang?"

"Nha Trang was a disaster. Everything was great until this morning. Then the young lady kicked me in the teeth. What's the situation?"

"Well, the Cong are hitting Ahn Tap…"

Gerber interrupted. "I know the background. Bates briefed me. What are we doing about it?"

"Bao has a company of strikers ready to go. I plan to take the first wave in with him as soon as we're loaded. Kepler will follow with the second, and Smith with the third, as soon as the aircraft arrive. We'll land northwest of the village. Once everybody's down, we'll form up on line and sweep into the village. Choppers will return here ASAP and pick up the second company. If we make contact, they can be flown in to reinforce or serve as a blocking force."

"Fine. Where's Minh?"

"He's out in the boat with Fetterman. They're about half a klick upstream from Ahn Tap."

"He's where?"

"He's with Fetterman. They're…"

"Never mind. You stay here. Bao, Schmidt, come with me."

"Ah, Captain…" Bromhead started to protest.

"Don't argue with me, Lieutenant. I am not going to leave this camp without an officer in charge. You let Minh go with Fetterman, you're elected to stay here."

"I didn't exactly let him go, sir. In fact, I advised against it. He just didn't take my advice."

"We'll talk about it later, Lieutenant. That's all." Gerber climbed back into the helicopter and motioned to the pilot. A moment later, the flight lifted, ran a short distance down the airstrip to gain speed, then climbed out and headed for Ahn Tap. Below them, Gerber could see reflected in the moonlight the second flight of helicopters, inbound for the camp.

CHAPTER 9

THE VILLAGE OF AHN TAP

The men in the motorboat watched helplessly as the village of Ahn Tap burned. The orgy of firing had tapered off to a sporadic crackling of rifles and carbines intermixed with an occasional burst from an AK, and people could still be heard yelling or screaming above the roar of the blazing huts, but there were not so many screams now, and very few yells.

Judging from the visible destruction, Fetterman estimated that the village had been hit by at least a reinforced company of Main Force Viet Cong. The volume of gunfire and the number of automatic weapons and rocket-propelled grenades indicated that they were far too well armed to have been local guerrillas.

It had chafed the men, Minh more so than the rest, to have to sit by and watch the carnage they knew was taking place in the village; there was nothing four men in a motorboat could do against such an obviously superior enemy force, not even four heavily armed men in a motorboat. Tonight, before their eyes, the village of Ahn Tap was dying, and they were powerless to do anything about it.

After a time, the effect of their inability to respond to the outrage had begun to make itself apparent in the unconscious actions of the men. Doc McMillan sorted through and repacked his medic bag three times. Sergeant Tyme repeatedly checked, unnecessarily, the ammunition belts and feed mechanisms of his twin .30-cal. Browning machine guns. Minh had put aside his rocket launcher, and sat nervously fixing and unfixing the bayonet to his heavy Garand rifle. Fetterman, who observed these behavioral tics in the others, failed to notice anything unusual in his own behavior until he caught himself checking the load in his M-79 for the fourth time.

At last the radio crackled with their call sign. Fetterman was surprised to find himself addressed by Gerber.

"Zulu Afloat, this is Zulu Six. We are two minutes out. Will land northwest of the village and sweep through toward the river. Can you establish a blocking position to the southeast, near the dock?"

Fetterman quickly considered the resources available to him. He had only four men, including himself, but they were armed with three machine guns, a grenade launcher, and a bazooka, as well as personal weapons. While it would have been foolish to attack a force the size of the one that must have hit Ahn Tap, it might be feasible for them to function as a partial block, provided they could get ashore undetected and find suitable cover.

"Roger Zulu Six. Will establish a blocking position near the dock. Out."

"Doc, clear the belt on that weapon, and bring the ammo. We don't have time to unbolt the tripod from the deck." Fetterman turned slightly to face Tyme. "Boom-Boom, dismount both those Brownings. Cut up the anchor line and rig a couple of slings. Lieutenant Minh, please bring the launcher and as many rockets as you can carry. We're going ashore."

Fetterman cut across the river at high speed and ran the little boat in alongside the dock.

Tyme leaped onto the boat dock, one of the big Brownings held ready in his hands, ammunition belt dangling, the weight of the weapon partially supported by the makeshift sling. He knelt on one knee, ready to provide covering fire while McMillan and Minh made the boat fast fore and aft, and Fetterman rapidly set ammunition boxes out on the dock. Then the three men scrambled out of the boat, and all four ran into the village. Huts and buildings were burning all around them, and a few bodies lay upon the ground, their limbs twisted into grotesque postures. Many of the bodies had obviously been badly burned.

They deployed in a ditch that paralleled the market, but was a street away. The marketplace itself would have offered the best field of fire, but it was so obvious that Fetterman figured only an idiot would try to cross it. Besides, anyone trying to get out of the village that way would still have to swing toward their position, or cross the river, and Fetterman could observe the boat dock from where he was.

The ditch had been used as an open sewer. It was partly full and stank to high heaven, but it offered the best protection available. Fetterman set up one of the machine guns as best he could, and put McMillan on the left with the grenade launcher so that he could also act as loader for the machine gun. The master sergeant then positioned Tyme about forty yards along the ditch to his right with the other machine gun. Minh dropped in on his left with the bazooka and half a dozen rockets. Then, while the Green Berets checked their M-14s, Minh fixed the bayonet to his Garand and laid half a dozen eight-round clips and two hand grenades out in front of him. They were as ready as they were going to be, and Fetterman wished he could notify Gerber, but the radio had been left behind in the boat so that they could carry the heavy weapons and extra ammunition.

As soon as the first company of strikers was on the ground, Gerber threw one platoon out to the northeast with Smith in charge as a blocking force. He was to be reinforced by the second company of strikers who would be coming in with Anderson, Kittredge, and Tran, the LLDB Intelligence specialist. The second company would bring two 60mm mortars with them, as well as Sergeants Tri and Tam, the two LLDB medical specialists, and a couple of strikers who had been trained as medics.

Gerber took the remaining three platoons from the first company, and, accompanied by Bao, Kepler, and Schmidt, immediately advanced on the village.

Kepler had thought it unwise to advance with only three platoons, particularly before the second company had arrived with mortar support. It seemed to him like a good way to get three platoons ambushed by what had to be a much larger force of VC. But Gerber had been adamant, and Kepler had worked with him long enough to know that when the captain had decided on a certain course of action, there was no sense trying to sway him from that course. Kepler shrugged and marked it off to concern on Gerber's part about catching the enemy before they could slip out of the village. It was, after all, the first time he could remember questioning the tactical soundness of an order the captain had given.

They advanced toward the village on line and swept through the rutted streets between the burning huts. The devastation was total. There was not a single hut that had not been set on fire. In the hamlet of Ahn Tap 1, nothing lived. Not even the pigs and chickens that had been penned up behind many of the homes. Curiously, there were few bodies, and no wounded. They checked the hamlet thoroughly, but found no one, nor were they fired upon.

In Ahn Tap 2, the story was much the same, except that here the few sturdy structures of stone or concrete had been blasted into rubble with explosives. There was no sign of the enemy, except for the destruction the Viet Cong had left behind them. Gerber moved his men quickly through the largest of the three hamlets, converging on the large, open marketplace, and eventually linked up with Fetterman's group. Together they swung to the northeast, toward Smith's blocking force which, by now, had been reinforced by the second company with the mortars and medical team. There were a few more bodies scattered about, mostly the very old or the very young — those who had been unable to run fast enough to escape the death overtaking them. All had been shot or bayoneted repeatedly, a few of the females had apparently been raped, their clothing ripped from their bodies; one was a girl who could have been no more than eight or ten years old.

McMillan was openly horrified at the carnage. He could not understand why there were no wounded. There should have been some who were only wounded.

Then, as they moved into Ahn Tap 3, they found the real horror.

In the smaller, old market there, now no longer used, they found the remaining citizens of the village of Ahn Tap. The Viet Cong had herded them into the square, shouting and shooting, panicking the frightened villagers headlong into the barbed wire barricades stretched across the far end. Then the VC had closed the trap behind them, and annihilated them. With flamethrowers.

There had been no wounded in the village of Ahn Tap because there were no wounded, only corpses charred beyond recognition.

There was, however, a single survivor.

Fetterman found him. He was huddled in the water beneath the boat dock, the only structure that remained intact in the village of Ahn Tap. A small, frightened boy, about eleven years of age, he was dressed only in a pair of pajama bottoms and was holding a small black puppy in his arms. When Fetterman approached the boy, he backed away and scrambled behind a piling. As he did so, the puppy's head lolled to one side. It was obvious that its neck was broken.

Fetterman stopped and slung his weapon over his shoulder, then, kneeling down in the water so that he would be on the boy's level, he held out his empty hands toward the boy, and tried the one sentence of Vietnamese he knew.

"*Dung so, chung toi la ban.* Don't be afraid son, we're friends. I promise I won't let anybody hurt you or your dog."

CHAPTER 10

MACV HEADQUARTERS, SAIGON

Lieutenant Colonel Alan Bates stood in the spartan outer office watching the clock on the wall. The grizzled old master sergeant behind the scarred and pitted steel desk watched it too. It was a familiar ritual. The two men had shared it seven days a week with very few exceptions for over half a year now. When the clock snapped from 0859 to 0900 the sergeant said, "You may go in now, sir."

Bates stepped to the door to the inner office, knocked three times, and waited a moment for the answer that had never been forthcoming in the one-hundred-and-ninety-odd times that he'd been through this before. After a long five-count, he pushed open the door, shuddering involuntarily as the frigid blast of the giant air conditioner washed over him like the wintry breath of a January day in his native state of Wisconsin, almost crystallizing the sweat stains in his jungle fatigues. Bates stepped quickly inside and softly closed the door behind him.

Across a vast expanse of new, thick, red shag carpeting, behind an opulent oak desk, Brigadier General Billy Joe Crinshaw sat in a high-backed leather armchair, wearing a field jacket. He was writing with a fourteen-carat gold Cross pen, and carefully ignoring the colonel. It was Crinshaw's little way of letting Bates know he was still the boss. There was no reason for it. It was just the general's traditional way of opening his morning briefing from Bates. Crinshaw had been doing it since he had become deputy chief of operations. And

Brigadier General Billy Joe Crinshaw was a strong-minded man when it came to traditions.

After exactly one full minute, Crinshaw put down his pen, looked up, and said the exact same thing he'd said one-hundred-and-ninety-plus times before. "Okay, Alan. What do you have?"

Bates moved to the easel set in one corner of the room. It held a large map stuck full of brightly colored pins showing the location of all American and South Vietnamese forces and of all known or suspected Viet Cong forces in the IV Corps operational area of Vietnam. The map, classified as "secret," was uncovered as usual. Bates, as he had done nearly two hundred times before, said nothing about the flagrant breach of security, but merely opened his leather briefing folder and began without preamble.

"Light contact has been reported within the last twenty-four hours near Tan-an, Vinh Tuy, and Phuoc Long, mostly ARVN units coming under intermittent sniper fire from local guerrillas. Camp A-552, that's over by Thot-not, was mortared again last night, that's nothing new, they get mortared every night."

As usual, Crinshaw interrupted him. "How do you know they were local guerrillas?"

"The snipers, you mean?"

"Yes. How do you know the snipers were local guerrillas? How do you know they weren't part of a larger, Main Force unit?"

It was the kind of question so obvious that only generals asked it. Bates felt a headache coming on. "In each case, only one or two Viet Cong were involved. They wore no uniforms, and were armed with outdated French MAS or Soviet Mosin

Nagant bolt-action rifles. Further, we have no reports of Main Force Viet Cong units operating in those areas at this time."

Crinshaw nodded as if it were exactly the answer he had expected. "Continue."

"Outside of IV Corps, the enemy has continued his gradual build-up around Hue and in the Tay Ninh area. This assessment is based on the increasing frequency with which our patrols and those of the ARVN have been encountering VC patrols over the last two weeks. There was light contact in both these areas again last night. Although no confirmed kills were counted after the engagements, several blood trails were found and eleven weapons were captured."

"What sort of weapons?" Crinshaw wanted to know.

Bates glanced around the room before answering. The walls of Crinshaw's office were hung with a collection of rifles, carbines, submachine guns, and even a Tokarev pistol. Each weapon was mounted on a mahogany board with a small brass plaque identifying the weapon and telling where and when it had been captured. None of them, Bates knew, had been captured by Crinshaw.

Bates consulted a list from his briefing materials. "Nine rifles, a PPSh-41 SMG, and an SKS carbine."

"Oh. No machine guns?" Crinshaw seemed disappointed.

"No sir."

"Oh well. Go on."

"As discussed at last Friday's briefing," said Bates, touching the map briefly, "we put Captain Henderson's team into this area here, east of Dak To, early this morning to establish the new camp."

Crinshaw nodded absently and Bates hurried on, thankful that he wasn't going to have to justify the new camp all over again, as he had already done so many times. It seemed he'd had to do that with every new camp the Special Forces had established since last May, when A-555 had been constructed.

"Coming back a bit closer to home, patrols along the Mekong river reported a significant increase in sampan traffic by the Viet Cong, although travel by the locals is down. This ties in with intelligence estimates that a major build-up is underway in the delta region, and that the focal points for a spring offensive will likely be in the Sa Dec and Go Cong areas, and possibly also in the inter-river regions between the Mekong and Bassac, north of Long Xuyen near Cho Moi. Reports from Naval Advisory Group also indicate that coastal patrols believe there's been an upswing of junk traffic in the Vinh Rach Gia region. The Navy is keeping their eye on the situation."

"God damn and the devil take the Navy," Crinshaw suddenly exploded. "Those incompetent sonsofbitches couldn't find the battleship *New Jersey* if she were tied up to the Saigon pier and firing off a twenty-one gun salute."

"Oh?" said Bates mildly. "I didn't know the Navy had lost a battleship. Where did they lose it?" Bates knew he was skating on thin ice, but he just couldn't resist the opportunity to twist the knife.

Crinshaw glared at him, unable to say what he wanted to without divulging that he had illegally had a motorboat shipped to Vietnam from the States aboard a U.S. Navy cargo vessel, for his personal use.

"That was a metaphorical statement, Colonel. What I meant was that our Naval colleagues seem to have difficulty remembering where they've put things."

Bates continued to play the straight man. "Oh, I see. They haven't actually lost a battleship then. What did they lose, some other kind of boat?"

Crinshaw turned positively purple. He made a small, strangled sound. His teeth clenched and he felt blindly about his desk top for the gold pen.

Bates decided he'd had his fun, and had better wrap things up while he still had Crinshaw on the defensive. A lot depended on his timing right now. Things were moving so fast that he hadn't had time to discuss with Gerber the outcome of his meeting with General Hull and Admiral Speas. The captain had rushed back to camp A-555 too soon. It would be at least a week, perhaps two, before the plan Bates had discussed with Hull and Speas could be put into operation, so there would still be plenty of time for Gerber to be informed and make the necessary arrangements at his end. However, if Crinshaw didn't react the way Bates needed him to in the next five minutes, none of it would make any difference. The moment of truth had arrived.

"There is just one more item for you to be aware of, General," said Bates. "Last night a large force of Viet Cong, perhaps an entire battalion, attacked and destroyed the village of Ahn Tap, inflicting extremely heavy civilian casualties."

"Why didn't you tell me about it first? Damn it, man, why didn't you tell me about it last night?"

Bates knew he'd had no obligation to inform Crinshaw of the action last night. Crinshaw was not his direct line superior, but was in a position to control most of the supplies the Green Berets needed, and wielded considerable influence over which of their operations received approval to go ahead. Bates knew better than to point out the lack of obligation.

"It wasn't really a military operation from our standpoint, General. We took no casualties and never did make contact with the enemy. We did have a small reconnaissance patrol in the area, but they were unable to maintain observation of the enemy, and the VC had escaped by the time we could get some helicopters out there and lift in a reaction force."

"You say the enemy slipped away before our people could get there. How did the Cong manage to do that?"

"The village itself sits right on the river, General. The surrounding area is mostly swamp verging on rain forest, with the only clear areas cultivated paddies immediately around the village. It's not a good place for helicopters to operate, especially at night. There's only one road through the area, which is impassable about five months of the year and mined by the VC during the other seven. The whole place is honeycombed with streams, canals, and ditches, making cross-country travel extremely difficult. The local Intelligence specialist out there theorizes that the VC may have used a combination of foot movement and sampans to slip out of the village. We do know that the VC have been making extensive use of the waterways in the area to bring in supplies from Cambodia. We've sunk a bunch of VC shipping out there with riverbank ambushes, including that group of ten sampans I told you about last week."

"Hmmm, yes. That was Gerber's bunch, wasn't it?"

"That's correct, General. They've been doing a bang-up job for you out there, in spite of those supply problems you foresaw so clearly when we put Camp A-555 out there." Bates knew he was overdoing it, but figured that with Crinshaw, it wouldn't hurt to grease the wheels a bit.

"Yes. Well, I suppose they are a good bunch of soldiers at heart. I do worry about Captain Gerber though. His thinking is just a bit too unconventional at times, if you take my meaning. Just where, exactly, is this Ahn Tap place?"

Bates pointed to a tiny dot on the map. "Right here, or at least it was. There's not much of it left now."

Crinshaw eyed the map. "Say, you know, that's only about ten miles from Cho Moi, practically in the Plain of Reeds. Isn't that where you said Intell estimated one of the focal points for the Cong's big build-up was located."

"Why yes, General, I believe you're correct," Bates answered with a perfectly straight face.

"Tell me, Alan, why do you suppose the Cong went in there and leveled that village last night?"

"Well, General, Gerber's men sank that big sampan convoy because of information provided them by the village chief of Ahn Tap. I suppose the massacre out there was intended as a warning to the other villages in the region not to cooperate with the Americans."

"Yes, yes," said Crinshaw excitedly, "but you're missing the meat of it, Alan. And let's not use the word massacre. It has such a bad ring to it in the press."

"I'm still not with you, General." Bates was, in fact, way ahead of him.

"Look here, boy, don't you see what's going on? Of course Ahn Tap was meant to be an example to the other villages, but why such an extreme example? There's only one possible explanation for it. It's critical to the Cong to keep the peasants paralyzed with fear right now so that they won't give away information about their build-up in the area. The boys in Intell are right. Charlie's getting ready for something big, and Gerber and his boys are smack in the middle of it. Now the question is, what can we do about it? How can we get Gerber and his bunch into a position where they can catch old Charlie with his pants down, and give him a kick in the ass?"

"Well, General, one of the things we'd have to do is reinforce Camp A-555. Right now Gerber's got two full companies of Tai strikers and two companies of RFs, but you know as well as I do that RF companies are only about half the size of a normal company. He'd have to leave most of them behind just to man the camp's defenses. I'd say he'd need at least two more companies if he's going to mount the kind of major break-up operation you're talking about."

"Hmmm, well, you've got a Tai strike company with Petersen's bunch out at Moc Hoa, don't you? How about transferring them out there on a temporary basis? Things have been fairly slow in Petersen's area for a while now, haven't they?"

"Well, yes, I suppose we could do that, but that still leaves us about... Say, wait a minute. Henderson just finished a training stint with an ARVN Ranger company. If we could arrange to borrow those Rangers for a couple of weeks we just might..."

"That's the spirit, boy. Now you're thinking like Regular Army. General Kien and I play tennis every Friday morning. I'll speak to him about loaning us some of his Rangers tomorrow morning."

It was time to take the big plunge. Bates hoped he could keep a straight face. "Oh what's the use, General. We've still the transportation problem, and fielding an operation like this would put an awful strain on your supply people. They're having a hard enough time just keeping Gerber's men armed and fed, without adding all those extra men."

"Damn the supply problems, boy. I'll see to it that they get everything they need if I have to have my people carry it out to them on their backs."

"That's very kind of you, General, but I still don't see how we're going to get around the transportation problem, and then there's fire support to consider. Just a million little things. The big problem is the transportation, though. I just don't see how we could operate that many helicopters in the Cho Moi area, even if we had them. The ground is just too soft, and there's all those damned canals and creeks and tributaries, and it's right smack between the Bassac and the Mekong."

Crinshaw leaned back in his chair, scratched his nose, and lit up a cigar. He didn't offer one to Bates. "I suppose you're right, Alan. It doesn't do us any good to have the men if we can't move them into contact with the enemy. Still, it was a pretty fair idea."

Crinshaw seemed to forget the whole notion as quickly as he'd thought of it under Bates's careful direction. "You got anything else for me today?"

Bates carefully closed his folder and covered the map. "No. That concludes today's briefing, General. I'll have a written report in your box by thirteen hundred hours."

Crinshaw nodded, picked up his pen, and began writing again. It was his way of telling Bates he could go.

Bates let himself out. The temperature change from Crinshaw's inner sanctum to the outer office was like walking into a foundry, soaking him instantly with sweat. He leaned with his back up against the door for a moment and breathed a sigh of relief. Then he walked slowly back across the compound to his own office, picked up the battered old telephone from his battered old desk, and placed a call.

"General Hull," he said, when the call went through, "this is Lieutenant Colonel Bates. That idea we discussed with Admiral Speas night before last? I think you might want to give General Crinshaw a call about it later this morning. I believe you might find him unusually receptive to the idea. Yes, General, I'm almost positive of it. Thank you, General. Yes, I'll be in my office all afternoon. Thank you again, General. Goodbye."

CHAPTER 11

SPECIAL FORCES CAMP A-555

By late afternoon, things had finally quieted down enough for Gerber to get back to camp and start preparing the after-action report on the Ahn Tap massacre that would be required by the Saigon command. Once again, he found himself in the position of having to falsify part of the report in order to cover up the fact that his men had been patrolling in a stolen boat. It wasn't really a question of lying, just of leaving out certain information that really didn't have a direct bearing on the operation anyway. Try as he might, Gerber still couldn't justify it to himself. He'd been raised to place a premium on honesty, to tell the truth and take the consequences no matter what. Now his childhood idealism had become just another casualty of the war in Vietnam.

Lieutenant Minh and Sergeants Kepler and Tran had questioned the sole survivor of the massacre at length after Doc McMillan had pronounced the boy healthy. They had learned almost nothing.

The boy's name was Le Quan Kim. He spoke Vietnamese, some French, and a very little English. He had been taught to read a little and to write his own name by the schoolteacher who had lived in the village for a few months before the Viet Cong killed her, and by one of the old men in the village who had been educated in Can Tho. He did not know who had attacked the village except that it had been the Viet Cong. He did not know how many Viet Cong had attacked the village, except that there had been a great many of them. He did not know how many people the Viet Cong had killed, except that they had tried to kill everyone they saw, and that after a while all the killing made them crazy and they started killing the dogs and pigs and even the chickens.

Le said he thought he had seen some of the Viet Cong before, perhaps when the VC had come into the village to purchase or tax food supplies from the villagers or deliver political lectures, but he could not be certain. Then he dropped a small bombshell. The Viet Cong, he said, had been accompanied by a Chinese officer.

At the mention of the Chinese officer, Fetterman had flown into such a rage that Gerber had to order him confined to his quarters for the rest of the day.

Gerber understood Fetterman's anger. The mysterious Chinese had been in the area advising local Viet Cong units since Camp A-555 was established. His path had crossed those of the American Special Forces soldiers several times, and always he had proved to be a thorn in their sides. But the situation had almost developed into a vendetta with Fetterman. Gerber had considered the notion that Fetterman might set out after the man on his own a real possibility.

After that, there had been the ugly scene with the journalists. The Saigon press commandos had somehow gotten wind of what had happened at Ahn Tap, and a team of reporters and photographers had shown up by helicopter about noon. They'd done nothing but question the obvious and get in the way of those involved in the clean-up operation or in trying to sort out what had happened and where the VC had gone. Gerber had finally ordered them out of the area when he'd discovered one of the photographers trying to get a group of Tais to pose with their weapons over the bodies of some of the villagers.

Gerber was tired. He'd been up now for almost thirty-six hours straight. He needed a shower and some sleep. Instead, he was making do on coffee that always seemed to be too hot to drink, or cold enough to freeze the back end of a polar bear. He'd lost track of how many cups.

He also needed some time to just sit down and try to make some sort of sense out of the events of the last few days, to try to understand what had gone wrong in Nha Trang just when everything seemed to be going so good. Despite the incident of the high casualty day at the hospital, he'd thought everything was okay between Karen and himself. In fact, after the incident in the bar, he'd felt closer to her than he had at any time in their relationship, closer than he'd ever felt with a woman before. He'd believed those feelings were returned. Then, yesterday morning, she'd abruptly announced that she didn't think the relationship was going to work out, and that she didn't want to see him anymore, at least for a while. When he'd tried to talk to her about it, she'd gotten angry and walked out.

Gerber had sat on the bed in the room they'd shared in the Regence for nearly two hours after she'd gone, wondering what in the hell he'd done wrong. Finally, he'd packed up his gear, checked out, and gone to the airfield where he could catch a flight to Saigon, cutting his R and R short by a day. He'd been at Tan Son Nhut, waiting for the next morning's supply flight out to his camp and drinking a bit more than he should have been in the officers' club when he bumped into Colonel Bates. They'd barely had time to say hello when Sergeant Taylor showed up to tell them the B-team TOC had received a message from Gerber's XO that something was going down in Ahn Tap. After that, Gerber hadn't had time to feel sorry for himself. It was a temporal luxury he simply couldn't afford.

Now, things were winding down, and as the professional pressure eased off, the personal pressures were making a comeback. Gerber couldn't believe how much it hurt. He'd had love affairs before that hadn't worked out, one or two of them even fairly serious. The predominant feeling on those occasions had been one of disappointment. But this one felt like someone had chopped his arm off. Even the sucking chest wound he'd gotten in Korea hadn't been this bad. He told himself that he was making too much out of the situation, that the lady was obviously screwed up, a poor choice for a serious relationship, and that the smartest thing he could do was forget her as quickly as possible. He told himself the hurt he was feeling now was only anger turned inward, anger at being lied to, used. He told himself that Karen was the one with the problem, not him. It didn't help. The truth was, the problem was his. She could say goodbye, and he couldn't.

There was a knock at the door, and Gerber looked up to see Bromhead. "Come on in, Johnny. What do you need?"

Bromhead marched into the hootch, stopped centered in front of Gerber's ammo crate desk, and saluted stiffly. "Sir, Lieutenant Bromhead requests permission to speak with the Captain."

"What is this saluting horseshit? And since when did you ever need to request permission to speak with me?" said Gerber with some surprise. "You know my door's always open. Pull up a seat and tell me what you want."

"If it's all the same to you, Captain, I think I'd rather stand," said Bromhead. "I'd like to talk to you about my decision to allow Lieutenant Minh to accompany Master Sergeant Fetterman on patrol in the boat last night."

"Oh for Christ's sake, is that what this is all about?" Gerber threw down his pencil and pointed toward an empty ammo crate near the wall. "Lieutenant, pull up a chair and sit down. That's an order."

"Very well, sir." Bromhead was trying hard to maintain a formal attitude, but there was just a trace of puzzlement showing in his voice.

Gerber sighed and rubbed the stubble on his chin. "Look, Johnny, Minh shouldn't have insisted on going, you shouldn't have let him, and I shouldn't have jumped your ass the way I did. I'm sorry. You're a damned good soldier, and you've been a good friend, and I don't want to lose either your friendship or your professional advice over this. Minh was wrong, and you were wrong, and I handled it wrong. As far as I'm concerned the incident is forgotten.

"Now then, if I know you, you probably came in here to request a transfer. Well Lieutenant, you can forget it, because I won't approve it and I won't forward it. You can't just throw in the towel because the boss chews your ass once in a while. Even if the boss is a grouchy old sonofabitch.

"So. Did you have something you wanted to say to me?" Gerber finished.

"Yes sir," said Bromhead. "I didn't come in here to quit. I came in here to apologize. I should have been more forceful in advising Lieutenant Minh not to go.

"Also, I'd like to convey a request from Sergeant Fetterman that he be allowed to leave the team bunker for the purpose of helping the boy bury his dog. He said to tell you if you'd let him, he promises not to try to sneak off and kill that Chinese bastard."

Gerber smiled weakly. "Those his exact words?"

"No sir," answered Bromhead. "I believe his exact words were that motherfuckin' Chinese bastard."

"Tell Fetterman I believe him, and if he's lying to me I'll write Mrs. Fetterman a long letter telling her what a bad boy he's been. And then tell him I'll restrict him to quarters for a month if he ever acts up like that again.

"Anything else?"

"Disposition of night patrols, sir."

"What do you have in mind?" asked Gerber.

"Kepler figures the VC will be active tonight. Probably want to do a little boasting about how they made an example of the traitors in Ahn Tap right under the noses of the big bad Americans. Charlie was drawing a lot of food supplies out of Ahn Tap that the other villages in the area are going to have to make up for now. The Cong have got themselves in a tight spot. They had to make an example out of Ahn Tap because the village turned against them. At the same time, they lost a significant part of their base of support in this area. They're going to have to start putting the squeeze on the other villages pretty quickly.

"I thought I might let Kepler take the new guy, Schmidt I mean, over to Cai Thoi and scope out the situation. They can take a few of the Tais with them, people with combat experience. That way if they run into anything interesting, it might give Schmidt a chance to get his feet wet. Might send Sergeant Smith along with them. Sully and Kepler together ought to be able to keep Schmidt from getting zapped if he gets in over his head.

"I figured to send the boat crew down toward Cho Moi. It's a bit far, but it's the next river town down from Ahn Tap, and I don't think that Charlie's going to be going back there."

Gerber nodded. "Who's the crew tonight?"

"Same as last night, except Anderson replaces McMillan, and of course sir, I'll get one of the RFs to replace Lieutenant Minh."

"That would mean Fetterman and Tyme, wouldn't it? I'm not sure that's such a hot idea," mused Gerber.

"Master Sergeant Fetterman's the only person we have who seems to understand Chrysler outboards, sir," Bromhead defended his choice. "If they're going to be that far afield, I really think he should go. Besides, he and Sergeant Tyme work well together, and Anderson is pretty green yet. Not as green as Schmidt, but still pretty green. And anyway, that's pretty much the way our manpower distribution breaks down based on sleep, or lack thereof, that the men have had."

"Okay Johnny, but you make it clear to Fetterman that I am not providing him with an excuse to go looking for the Chinese guy. He's to conduct a routine combat patrol. Period. Understood?"

"Yes sir," answered Bromhead. "I'll make sure he understands. Sergeant Fetterman is a professional sir. If you'll pardon my saying so, you should try to remember that. I don't think he'd allow his personal feelings to interfere with his duties."

The subtlety of Bromhead's statement was not lost on Gerber. He glanced sharply at his executive officer, but Bromhead's face betrayed no hint that he might have intended a double meaning.

"I'm sure you're right, Johnny," said the captain, "and I'll try to remember that. I only hope Sergeant Fetterman remembers it too. Now how about getting out of here so I can finish this report before supper."

When Bromhead had gone, Gerber sat quietly for a moment, considering. He wondered whether he was just being paranoid, or had Bromhead really been trying to tell him something? He knew well enough what that something was, but he was unwilling to admit it. He was the commanding officer, the man who was supposed to hold the team together and make it run, the career professional who was supposed to be able to put considerations of mission success above all else. He was the hardened expert, grown so used to the killing that he could contemplate it in an almost casual manner, grown perhaps too used to it.

So why in the hell wasn't he acting like a professional? He'd chewed out his second in command for making a decision that, although wrong, really wasn't Bromhead's fault, and he'd made a decision of his own that had been both stupid and dangerous. He should never have taken a company of strikers into Ahn Tap last night without waiting for the second company to land with reinforcements and mortar support. For all he knew, there could have been a whole battalion of Viet Cong in the village. From the looks of things, there might well have been a whole battalion. And he hadn't even gone in there with a full company, just a couple of platoons. It had been a mistake, and it could have been a disaster. He realized that now.

And he also realized that Kepler had realized that last night and tried to talk him out of it. He was making judgmental errors, and in combat, that could prove fatal. It wasn't his own life that concerned Gerber. In fact, right now he was wondering whether staying alive was really worth all the trouble and effort, but he knew he had no right to risk the lives of men who trusted him. Not without good cause. They all accepted that risk daily, but they were entitled to expect that Gerber wouldn't throw their lives away, to expect that if some of them had to die, there would at least be a good reason for it.

And it was apparent to Gerber that more than one of his men realized that he wasn't using good judgment. More than one of them had seen that their captain was allowing problems in his personal life to affect the making of decisions that could end their lives.

Gerber knew he was going to have to do something about it. He even knew what. What he didn't know was how. They don't teach you how to psychoanalyze yourself in the Army. They teach you how to kill. The Army isn't interested in how you cope with your personal problems, only in how well.

And a bullet doesn't care that you got in front of it because your mind was working overtime trying to figure out why the woman you were going to marry decided to rip your heart out and stomp on it, when your mind should have been working on staying out of the bullet's way.

A bullet doesn't even care that you're dead.

A bullet doesn't...

A bullet.

CHAPTER 12

THE JUNGLE NEAR CAI THOI

Kepler and Smith weren't quite sure what to make of the FNG. Schmidt was weird. That much they could agree upon. Fetterman was weird, although no one questioned his professionalism when it came to combat, but compared to Schmidt, Fetterman was merely eccentric.

Nobody ever saw Schmidt except in his black jungle fatigues and black VC web gear. Nobody ever saw Schmidt without his poncho-liner blanket cape and M-60 machine gun. Nobody ever saw Schmidt without his black-rimmed sunglasses protecting, he said, his visual purple "from the blazing rays of Coleman lanterns and cigarette lighters." But what was really weird was that nobody ever saw Schmidt in the daylight.

Bocker claimed that Schmidt was just going to extremes to protect that super night vision of his, and that he spent the daylight hours sleeping in the darkest corner of the commo bunker where he'd rigged a curtain out of a poncho and hung it over his hammock like some kind of burial shroud, but nobody but Bocker had ever claimed to have actually seen Schmidt sleep. When they went to look for him in the sepulchral swinging bed, he was never there, and never anywhere else that anyone could find him. Schmidt was always up and about immediately after sundown however, so the men accepted Bocker's story about his sleeping during the day to protect his night vision. It went against the evidence of their own eyes, but it was a whole lot easier on the nerves than giving serious consideration to the alternative.

There was more to the mystery of Sergeant Vladimir T. Schmidt. He didn't, for instance, make any noise when he walked, despite the heavy M-60. No noise at all. And he could take three steps away from you in the night, even a fairly bright, moonlit night, and turn invisible, just simply vanish from sight. Fetterman claimed that there was nothing particularly remarkable about that. All it took was years of practice.

But the most damning piece of evidence against Schmidt was the way he shaved. He didn't use a mirror.

That last bit had made even Fetterman a bit uncomfortable. It wasn't that anybody actually believed Schmidt might really be a... The word was too creepy to even think about, let alone say. It wasn't as if anyone actually believed it, but it was true that the Tais were afraid of him. They wouldn't go near him unless they had to, and the Catholics among them always crossed themselves when they did.

None of the Green Berets would dream of doing anything so ridiculous as that, of course, especially not if they thought any of the other men might see them, but a few of them had taken to carrying tiny copies of the New Testament in the breast pocket of their jungle fatigues.

Yet Schmidt seemed friendly enough. A bit reserved perhaps, but that was normal enough when a new guy came into an established unit. And Bocker said he knew radios like Casanova knew women. And Tyme had watched him take apart his M-60, clean and inspect it, and put it back together in half the time it would have taken most experienced gunners. So maybe he was just a FNG who just happened to be a little weird.

Maybe.

In any event, Schmidt really did have fantastic night vision. There was a heavy overcast tonight, accompanied by thick ground fog. Kepler and Smith, by this time both old hands at night-time jungle patrols, had a hard time moving through the pea soup without tripping over a vine or walking into a branch every fifty to seventy-five yards. Schmidt moved through the stuff like he had radar. When it finally got so bad even the Tai striker walking point for their eight-man patrol couldn't tell where he was going, Kepler called a halt.

"This shit really sucks," whispered Smith.

"I know," Kepler said. "I hope Fetterman's bunch has better luck than we are. I can't see a fucking thing."

"So what are we going to do about it?"

"As I see it, we don't have much choice. We'll have to set up in a defensive circle and wait."

"For how long?"

"Until things clear. Until morning if necessary. At this point, I don't even think I could find our way back to camp," Kepler admitted. "I've been counting pace and keeping track of the compass bearings, but I can't find anything that even looks like a landmark. We could be less than a hundred meters from Cai Thoi right now, and walk right on past it in this stuff."

"There is an alternative, Sergeant Kepler," said Schmidt, and before either of them could stop him, he stepped half a dozen feet off the trail and did his vanishing act.

"Schmidt!" Kepler hissed. "Schmidt, Goddamnit, you come back here!"

"Christ! Now what are we going to do?" groaned Smith.

"The same thing we were going to do. We wait. But I'll tell you one thing, Sully, if I ever get my hands on that crazy bastard, I'm personally going to drive a wooden stake through that chicken-livered heart of his."

Inside of five minutes, Schmidt had returned, appearing suddenly out of the fog at Kepler's elbow and nearly giving him a heart attack.

"Your estimate of our position was a bit off, Sergeant, but remarkably good considering the weather conditions," said Schmidt simply.

"What the hell are you talking about?"

"The village of Cai Thoi. We're actually about two hundred meters southeast of it. There's a small trail about a dozen yards through the bush behind you that comes out behind an abandoned hootch on the outskirts."

"Well I'll be damned," said Smith.

"No, not yet," Schmidt replied obliquely. "Shall we go, gentlemen?"

They followed Schmidt through the brush for about fifteen steps and came out on the trail as promised. Weapons ready in case of ambush, they moved along it quickly, crossing through the mounded-up earth of an old cemetery before coming out at the back of the hootch. They sidled up against the flimsy structure and Smith leaned over to whisper in Kepler's ear.

"Leave it to Schmidt to find a path running through a graveyard."

"I'm just pleased that he could find a path," whispered Kepler.

Slowly, they worked their way among the houses, keeping to the shadowed areas beneath the thatched eaves. Although it was still fairly early, people weren't moving about because the weather was so lousy. Kerosene lanterns glowed in a few of the huts where people were still up visiting or playing cards or checkers, but most of the houses were dark, although the voices of the occupants could be heard through the open windows as people lay talking in their beds, or sat in the darkness, waiting to become tired. As they passed one particular house, Kepler held up a restraining hand, then slipped back to converse with Smith and Schmidt.

"The guys inside this house are VC. I overheard them talking about Ahn Tap. Evidently, the VC grapevine has preceded us. These guys are just local guerrillas. I suppose whoever hit Ahn Tap got the word out somehow to the VC agents in the villes, and they're supposed to spread the word around. These guys are talking about how to do it. Seems to be an argument between one guy who wants to make a big formal announcement in the marketplace tomorrow morning, and two other guys who think they ought to just start the story casually in conversation with a couple of people and let the village telegraph take care of the rest. I don't think they're too eager to publicly associate themselves with the Viet Cong this soon after the massacre. I think there might be a fourth guy in there too, but I'm not positive. He's not saying very much."

Smith nodded. "What do you think we ought to do about it?"

"I think it would be a hell of a deal if we could capture one of these guys for questioning. He might not be able to give us a whole lot of information, but even if we could just find out the name of the unit that hit Ahn Tap, that would give us a place to start. Besides, he's bound to have picked up some scuttlebutt about the build-up. We might even learn something important."

"Okay, how do you want to run it?"

"We'll deploy around the place and see what happens. If one of these guys decides it's time to go home to Mamasan, we'll put the bag on him. If they all decide to spend the night, we'll just have to wait until they go sleepy-by and go in and carry one of them out."

They deployed in a split semicircle about the house, Smith and three of the Tais covering the back of the hootch, Kepler, Schmidt, and the other two Tais covering the front. Then they settled down to wait.

They waited for the better part of two hours in the chill damp outside the hut, fighting off the sleep that comes from boredom. At last the kerosene lantern was extinguished and the house grew quiet. Kepler waited another hour to be on the safe side, then said, "I'm going to have a word with Smith," and crawled off. When he reached the rear of the house he looked around for Smith, but couldn't spot him, so he gave a low whistle. It was answered a few seconds later by the call of an owl, and Smith slid out from under a small, thorny-looking bush resembling a hedge, and motioned Kepler over to him.

"What's the scoop?"

"Looks like they've gone to bed. What do you think?"

"Yah. Must not have been anything good on Carson tonight," Smith quipped. "How do you figure to play this?"

"We'll leave Schmidt and the Tais out here to keep an eye on things while you and I slip in the back window. We'll pick the nearest VC, persuade him to come along quietly, and leave the way we came in."

"And if he doesn't want to come along quietly?" asked Smith.

"Then we'll just have to persuade him a little more vigorously, and run to beat hell. You got your persuader on you?"

Smith fished into one of the pockets of his jungle fatigues and produced a large, flat sap. He showed it to Kepler, who grinned, nodded, and produced his come-along, a ring-handled garrote with a thick piece of nylon parachute line instead of a piano wire. It was designed to incapacitate, not kill, although it could do so if applied long enough.

"Okay," said Kepler. "I'll go let Schmidt know what the situation is. Watch for me. When you see me crawl around the corner of the hootch, come on up and we'll get it on. You can have the privilege of going through the window first."

"Gee, thanks," grumbled Smith.

"Okay then, I'll stand in the middle of your back and you can boost me inside."

"No thanks. I'll go first. You've been eating too many C-rations lately."

Kepler snorted. "Look who's talking. You've been eating too much pasta for the last twenty-five years."

"It's only been twenty-four years, and it hasn't been nearly enough. Pasta is what makes all us Italians such great lovers. Everybody knows eating C's makes you sterile."

"Just be ready when I get back here, okay?" Kepler crawled away.

About five minutes later Kepler reappeared, but motioned to Smith to stay put. He then crawled over to the demolitions expert.

"Sully, get your men together and let's get the hell out of here. Right now."

Smith didn't question the sudden change in plan. If Kepler had decided it was time to leave, he'd have a good reason for doing so. Smith made a clucking sound, like one of the local lizards, and the three Tais immediately broke cover and moved in from their respective positions.

"What's the rush?" Smith finally asked as they crawled back around to the front to join Schmidt.

Kepler jerked a thumb in Schmidt's direction. Lying on the ground next to the new communications specialist was a Vietnamese, his wrists, ankles, and elbows tied together, and a tennis ball shoved into his mouth.

"Schmidt was busy while you and I were talking," said Kepler.

"Far out," said Smith. "Boy, those other guys sure will be surprised when they wake up and find their buddy here missing."

"Somehow, I don't think so. Isn't that right, Schmidt?"

"Huh?" interrupted Smith. "What do you mean by that?"

"What he means, Sergeant Smith," said Schmidt, "is that those other guys won't be waking up. Shall we go, gentlemen?"

CHAPTER 13

SONG TIEN GIANG, NEAR CHO MOI

The tiny, camouflaged motorboat crawled quietly along the north bank of the river, using the indistinct outline of the natural levee to keep from becoming lost in the dense fog. Twice they had become confused and turned into small coves by mistake anyway; still, it was better than trying to follow the south bank which was a veritable rabbit's warren of inlets, creeks, and canals. These smaller waterways connected with the Song Hau Giang or ran into smaller canals used to carry water to the villages and irrigate the fields and rice paddies.

The trip in the boat should have taken a little over an hour in good weather. It had already taken over three and a half hours because of the necessity of reducing speed in the fog; according to Fetterman's calculations, they were not quite there yet.

Fetterman mistrusted his own calculations to a certain degree. There had been no significant landmarks visible due to the fog, and even in good weather, he would have had to climb the riverbank for a closer look at the ones that he knew existed. Fetterman was using dead reckoning, relying on their known course and speed to tell them where they were, and he knew that the figures could be off by a fairly large margin due to changes in the river's course and time lost by the accidental detours into the two coves. He was counting on being able to see the diffuse glow of the lights of Cho Moi through the fog when they were opposite it.

Cho Moi was a good-sized town of several thousand population with a major canal connecting the Mekong and the shallower Bassac river to the south of it, although the principal trans-shipment point for traffic between the two rivers was farther south and east at Sa Dec, a city of about fifty thousand. Intelligence reports had indicated, however, that it was Cho Moi that was being used by the Viet Cong as a staging area for their build-up of weapons and supplies prior to an offense in the early spring. The Viet Cong had been bringing supplies in from North Vietnam and China, mostly via Cambodia, aboard shallow draft sampans capable of navigating either river, and Cho Moi provided a natural point of convergence sufficiently far removed from major population areas to escape serious attention or reaction from the Saigon government.

After much discussion, it had been decided that Sergeant Tri, the senior LLDB medical specialist, would go along as a fourth crew member in place of one of the strikers. This fulfilled the requirement of having a Vietnamese involved in the patrol, and provided medical support for the mission, as McMillan had the night before. At the last moment, Sergeant Tran, Minh's Intelligence specialist, had joined the crew as fifth member. While this made for crowded conditions aboard the craft, it provided the opportunity for a two-pronged mission.

Tran and Tri had both dressed in civilian clothes, and each carried a pistol and two hand grenades beneath his shirt. Tri had taped a combat knife to the inside of his left leg, and Tran had secured a switchblade to the inside of one arm in a similar fashion. Tri also had a large, nondescript, canvas shoulder bag that held two M-3 submachine guns and several magazines of ammunition. When they reached Cho Moi, Fetterman would land them near the waterfront, and the two Vietnamese would make their way into town and hang around at a couple of the local bars to see if they could pick up any useful gossip about the raid on Ahn Tap, or the suspected build-up.

Fetterman, Tyme, and Anderson would then patrol a few of the canals and coves in the motorboat, refuel the outboard's gas tanks from some premixed fuel brought along in jerry cans, and take up position off the public docks where they could watch for any suspicious shipping. At 0330 hours, they would return and pick up the Vietnamese soldiers, then make their way back upstream to the camp.

About twenty minutes after Fetterman figured they should be opposite Cho Moi, Tran thought he detected a vague luminescence off their starboard bow, and they cut across the river channel to the opposite shore.

As they got closer, it became apparent they had overshot their target a bit and were coming in right under the docks. Since the visibility was poor and no one seemed to be about, Fetterman ran the boat in alongside the wharf and discharged his passengers, who scrambled up a highly unsafe-looking ladder and disappeared into the fog. Fetterman then backed the boat out into the river again, and turned upstream, working the coves and inlets along the shoreline.

At a little past midnight, they were a couple of miles to the north of Cho Moi.

They had been patrolling for two hours without finding anything interesting, and ran aground three times in shallow waters in the coves and canals. Fetterman decided it was time to return to the area of the waterfront, refuel, and then lay at anchor in the channel. If any vessels came downstream at this hour, they would be assumed to be Viet Cong, and would be stopped and searched. If they attempted to flee, they would be fired upon.

Fetterman was just about to turn the boat around when Tyme said he thought he could hear voices. Fetterman quickly cut the engine, and the motorboat drifted to a halt in the water as the men strained their ears, listening for the sound.

After a moment, Anderson whispered, "Over there, to the right."

They all listened a few seconds longer, and when the sound of voices came again, Fetterman restarted the boat and the crew went to action stations.

Fetterman steered the boat out into the channel and switched on the headlight. The fog reflected the beam back at them, but the light proved some help, as Fetterman had earlier taken the precaution of wrapping the lens of the headlamp with several layers of black electrical tape, leaving only a small slit for the beam so that the light tended to fan out in front of them in a broad band, instead of being completely dispersed by the fog. The effect was much like driving a car with the headlights set on low beam.

Suddenly, a huge shape loomed up before them out of the fog — a small, rivergoing junk. Although not nearly as big as the oceangoing variety used along the seacoasts of Vietnam, it was easily four or five times as large as the motorboat.

"*Dung lai! Hang di!*" Tyme hailed the boat, since he didn't know how to say "Heave to," in Vietnamese.

The junk responded with silence, and Tyme called again.

"*Dung lai! Dung lai! Cho toi coi can cuoc ong. Co may nguoi voi ong?*"

"What the hell was all that, Boom-Boom?" asked Fetterman.

"I told him to show us their I.D. cards, and asked how many people were with them."

"You told them to show us their I.D. cards?" Fetterman said unbelievingly. "Are you out of your mind, Boom-Boom?"

"Christ's sake, Fetterman, give me a break, will ya? I don't know how to say 'Stop and identify yourself or we'll sink you.' If you want to try it, go ahead."

There was another short silence from the junk, followed by excited whispering, and then more silence.

Suddenly Fetterman yelled, "Open fire! Fire! Fire!" and slammed the throttle full forward. The motorboat leaped ahead just as a rocket-propelled grenade burst astern, showering them with a geyser of water. Had Fetterman been three or four seconds slower, they would have been blown right out of the water.

As the boat roared past the junk, Tyme raked the deck railing with the twin .30-cal. Brownings, and Anderson pumped rounds into the wooden hull of the vessel with the bow-mounted machine gun.

Fetterman killed the headlight, plunging them into darkness, and brought the boat back around in a wide circle. A light machine gun had started firing at them from the junk as they raced away from it, and although the gunner had lost his target when Fetterman turned off the light, the muzzle flashes provided a nice beacon for Fetterman to home back in on. He bore down on the flickering gun barrel, and when the VC quit firing, Fetterman switched the light back on, illuminating the target for Anderson and Tyme. The three .30-cals roared to life again, punishing the wooden boat.

When Fetterman killed the headlight this time, the VC gunner had sense enough to stop shooting as well, and the Americans lost the junk in the fog.

For nearly five minutes, the two vessels played a deadly game of cat and mouse in the darkness. Finally, there was an explosion some fifty yards away as somebody with an RPG onboard the junk thought he saw something and took a gamble. Although the rocket left a trail of sparks behind it, in the blackness it was impossible to tell exactly where it had come from.

Fetterman responded by blanketing the suspected area with half a dozen rounds from the 40mm grenade launcher, but couldn't be sure if he'd hit anything, or even exactly where the grenades had fallen.

They went back to silently stalking each other. Occasionally, one vessel would fire a grenade or a burst of machine gun fire at where he thought the other might be, but apparently without results. Neither boat risked a long enough burst for the other to home in on the muzzle flashes.

When neither had betrayed its presence for several minutes, Fetterman finally decided that something would have to be done to break the stalemate or the junk would succeed in slipping away downstream in the murk. He had Anderson load up the bazooka while Tyme stood by on the twin machine guns, then he prepared two green-star-parachute flares for launching.

Fetterman removed the protective end caps from the two aluminum-cased flares, fitting them to the butt of each tube so that the firing pin built into the inner face of the cap would be positioned over the shotgun primer in the base. Then he checked the load in the M-79 and in his M-14 as well.

"Ready?" asked Fetterman.

"Let's do it," said Tyme.

"Get some," echoed Anderson.

Fetterman pointed one of the flares in what he hoped was the right direction, and struck the end cap sharply with the heel of his hand. It arced skyward with a whoosh. Before the flare had a chance to burst, Fetterman dropped the empty tube, snatched up the second launcher, and fired it to the left of the first.

The flares popped overhead, turning the fog into a milky green phosphorescence that was reflected back by the water's surface and multiplied until the entire world seemed made up of one vast void with both vessels floating eerily in an endless green-white sky.

"Anderson!" Fetterman yelled. "Hit 'em now!"

There was a loud roar from the rocket launcher, and a mountain of water erupted beneath the bow of the junk.

Tyme opened up with the twin machine guns again, walking his tracer lines onto the target. The water droplets in the fog diffracted the light from the flares and the reflection of the boats, casting ghost images so that there seemed to be half a dozen boats, some beneath each other or to the side, others crazily drifting upside down in the air. Tyme's tracers, and their ethereal doppelgangers, tore into all of them, sending splinters flying in a storm of wood chips that was part real, part illusory.

Anderson reloaded the rocket launcher and fired again, his strike landing amidships of the junk this time, but short of the target.

The VC had apparently had problems spotting the camouflaged motorboat at first, but had now sighted the flickering muzzles of Tyme's machine guns, and were returning a heavy volume of gunfire. Their green and white tracers crisscrossed with the red from the Brownings, now visible, now gone, depending upon the predominant colors from the flickering flares. The VC with the RPG got into the act again, but his aim was even worse than Anderson's, and he missed the motorboat by at least twenty yards.

Fetterman was lobbing out grenades as fast as he could load and fire the M-79.

Anderson finally succeeded in getting off a third round with the bazooka, and struck the rear of the junk, blowing off the poop deck in a great shower of timbers and burning phosphorous.

The victory was short-lived however, as a twelve-seven opened up from the foredeck of the junk, tearing ragged holes through the foggy air.

Realizing that in this instance discretion might well be the better part of valor, Fetterman engaged the prop and brought the throttle forward, intending to use the greater speed and maneuverability of the motorboat to flank the enemy. As they sped in toward the enemy, the flares dropped sizzling into the water, plunging the combatants back into darkness.

For a moment, both boats continued to fire at the muzzle flashes of the other. Then, as the aim of the VC gunner with the 12.7mm heavy machine gun began to become uncomfortably close, Tyme decided that fighting a duel against a heavy machine gun with two light machine guns was not such a hot idea. As the twin .30-cals fell silent, Anderson got off his fourth and final round with the 3.5-inch launcher. The rocket's flight was punctuated with a thoroughly satisfying explosion, but after an initial burst of brilliant white light, the junk was once again lost to view.

Fetterman cut power to the engine and searched frantically beneath the dashboard of the boat for another flare. At last he found one, removed the end cap, and fired it. As it popped dangling beneath the parachute, Fetterman glanced to the side and was horrified to see the junk bearing down directly upon them, its huge prow looming almost overhead.

"Enemy at three o'clock!" Fetterman yelled a warning to the others, and slammed the throttle forward.

The big Chrysler outboard coughed once and died.

The gas tank was empty.

Fetterman didn't waste time trying to restart the engine. He grabbed up his M-14, yelled "Abandon ship!" and dived over the side of the boat into the blood-warm waters of the Mekong. As the water closed over his head he could hear the grinding, rending crunch of heavy wooden timbers biting into thin fiberglass.

Fetterman dived deep, stroking to pull himself farther down as the junk passed overhead. At last, when he felt his lungs would burst if he stayed down a moment longer, he arched his back and let the stale air in his lungs carry him back to the surface, giving only an occasional stroke with his arms or kick with his feet. It almost didn't work.

He'd ditched his helmet as soon as he'd decided it was time to surface, but his heavy flak jacket and ammunition-weighted web gear were pulling him down. He glanced around for the junk, fully expecting to be riddled with machine gun bullets while he was exposed to the light of the flare, and sank beneath the surface once again.

Remembering that panic kills, Fetterman calmly hooked the sling of his rifle around one ankle. Then he unbuckled his web gear, put it between his feet, and held it there while he struggled out of the ten-pound flak vest. He let the vest drop away, bent his knees, and slipped one arm through the webbing of his combat gear, then fought his way to the surface. He popped out of the water gasping, sucked in two great lungfuls of air, then went under a third time to unstrap the rifle from his ankle. He passed the sling of the rifle through the belt of his pants, so that he could tow it more conveniently, and made it back up again. As he looked around this time, he could see the junk, a small fire burning on its rear deck, disappear into the fog as it continued downriver. He shouted for both Tyme and Anderson, calling their names, but there was no reply.

Fetterman experimented, and found he could float, after a fashion, by lying on his back. He did so, and opened the combat pack on his web gear, letting the extra ammunition and C-rations inside drop out into the river. He pulled the plastic liner out of the pack as far as it would go, then inverted it and swung it down into the water, trapping an air pocket inside. With the weight of the ammunition pouches on the web belt partially supported by the air in the butt pack, Fetterman was then able to get both canteens out of their covers, drain them, and replace them on the belt, giving two more air chambers, and making a sort of rudimentary life preserver.

The flare had sputtered out in the water by this time, leaving him in total darkness, and he had no way to judge which was the closest shore, but he could get a sense of which direction was downstream by the last sighting of the junk, and he struck out at a forty-five degree angle to that, not fighting the current, but letting it carry him along as he angled for the south bank.

At long last, and near exhaustion, he saw some lights slipping ahead of him, and realized that he had been swimming in the right direction. They were little more than indistinct glows in the distance, but they could only be lights from the town of Cho Moi. With a renewed sense of purpose, he once again swam hard, and eventually made it into shallows, collapsing in the mud at the base of the riverbank. He lay there for a long time, breathing heavily before he had the strength to claw his way up the slippery embankment.

Once over the levee on relatively dry land, Fetterman took inventory. He had, by keeping a calm head under stress, managed to retain his rifle, 140 rounds of ammunition, the snub-nosed .44 magnum revolver he carried in a shoulder holster beneath his jungle jacket, his web gear and poncho, and his prized Case VS-21 fighting knife. But the most valuable asset of all hung from a lanyard about his neck, his lensatic compass. A man could get out of any jungle, given enough time and a good compass, Fetterman knew. Slowly, however, the realization sank through to his fatigue-numbed brain. He didn't have to walk back to the camp through the jungle. All he had to do was walk as far as the wharf in Cho Moi.

As soon as he felt rested enough to travel, Fetterman started out. As he walked, he untaped the two extra magazines that were fastened to the one inserted in his M-14, and stuffed the spares into the pockets of his jungle jacket. It made the weapon easier to carry, and less cumbersome, should he have to use it.

He had been carried past Cho Moi by the river current, but easily found a wide path running alongside the embankment. It was obviously well used by the local population, and he followed it into the town, although it was difficult at times because of poor visibility.

Once in Cho Moi, he worked his way slowly toward the waterfront, keeping off major streets and in the shadows as much as possible. He moved with caution. He was the only American in a town of several thousand Vietnamese, some of whom would be loyal to the Saigon government, some of whom would be loyal to the Viet Cong. Except for the few broken phrases he had learned, he did not speak their language.

It was well after 0400 hours when he finally reached the rendezvous with Tri and Tran at the Cho Moi docks. The others were there as well.

Tyme had not been able to grab his rifle before going over the side, as he had been too busy firing the twin machine guns at the junk bearing down on them. He had managed, however, to retain his personal gear, including his 9mm pistol, and a couple of grenades. He'd found a seat cushion from the motorboat floating by while he was in the water, and used it to support himself like a kickboard, making his way to shore before his shipmates.

Anderson confessed that he'd been too excited to think of saving his rifle. Instead, he'd saved the bazooka and four rockets. The fiberglass bow of the boat, he explained, had stayed afloat after the collision, although it was upside down. He'd used it to float the big aluminum rocket launcher, which, although large, didn't weigh much, and had pushed the fractured piece of boat in to the shore. Later, he'd tried to salvage the .30-cal. machine gun that was bolted to the deck and now hung upside down in the water, but he'd been unable to get the weapon free of its mount.

"What about the junk?" asked Tyme.

"It was burning the last time I saw it," Fetterman told them. "I don't know if it sank or not. We must have scored several hits on it, but it didn't look all that badly damaged to me."

"Did you guys find out anything useful?" he asked Tran.

"Affirmative," said the Intell specialist. "Sergeant Tri and I drink beaucoup cold beers while you gentlemen try and drown yourselfs. We also listen to beaucoup talk. There beaucoup talk in town about Ahn Tap. Pretty much everybody say it one-twenty-ninth Main Force that hit Ahn Tap. They also say it Major Huynh Dong Long command one-twenty-ninth. Him former commander one-twenty-third. I think maybe there is no one-twenty-third anymore."

"Did you get any news of the build-up? Did anyone mention it?" questioned Fetterman.

"No one have to mention it," said Tran. "Half the people in bars VC. Some of them not even bother to change out of uniform. Cho Moi the place, all right. From conversation, I think VC have a major base about a klick from here on the Kinh Ky Canal. They must be awfully sure of selfs. They not try and hide it much."

"Great," said Fetterman. "Good work. We better get that information back to camp as soon as possible."

"And just how are we going to do that, send a carrier pigeon?" snorted Tyme.

"Well, Boom-Boom," answered Fetterman. "I suppose we could do it that way, but I sort of figured we'd just steal one of these sampans tied up to the pier here. If we hurry, we ought to be able to make it back to camp by lunchtime."

CHAPTER 14

B-TEAM HEADQUARTERS, SAIGON

It was exactly one week after Crinshaw's motorboat was sent to the bottom of the Mekong River by the Viet Cong junk when Gerber stepped off the Caribou transport at Tan Son Nhut and made his way to Lieutenant Colonel Bates's office.

A mysterious message from Bates the day before had instructed him to utilize an aircraft that would land at Camp A-555 to deliver supplies, for return to Saigon, and to have his communications personnel report his departure to Bates once Gerber was en route.

Gerber had expected the usual Delta model Huey that served as morning courier flight from Saigon and delivered such minor odds and ends as the camp needed to keep running. Instead, he'd got the Caribou and over three tons of C-rations he hadn't ordered. Puzzled, he'd complied with instructions, figuring Bates would tell him all about it when he got there.

Sergeant Taylor, Bates's administrative assistant, greeted him with a cheery "Good morning, sir. You can go right in. They're expecting you."

Gerber wasn't sure he liked the sound of that, but Taylor seemed in an upbeat mood, so he pushed the door open and strode right in.

The shock almost killed him.

Crammed inside Bates's tiny office were the Colonel, Major General Hull, Rear Admiral Speas from Naval Advisory

Group, and a lieutenant commander whom Gerber did not recognize.

My God, thought Gerber, they've found out about Crinshaw's boat.

"Morning, Mack," said Bates. "This is Admiral Speas and Lieutenant Commander Russell from NAG. I believe you know General Hull. Gentlemen, Captain Mackenzie K. Gerber, the man I told you about."

Bates called past Gerber through the open door. "Taylor, coffee in ten minutes. All right?"

"Certainly, Colonel, I'll have it ready."

"Well don't just stand there, Mack," smiled Bates. "Come on in and close the door. These gentlemen want to talk with you about something. I guess you could say it's all your fault. Have a seat."

Gerber sank gratefully into the chair. His knees felt weak, and he felt like he was going to be sick. He'd always known that sooner or later the axe would fall, but he hadn't expected it to come like this. Why was Bates grinning like a maniac?

Everyone waited expectantly for a moment to see who would speak first. Finally, both Speas and Bates nodded at the General, who cleared his throat.

"I'm going to dispense with the captain business, Mack. You and I went through jump school together way back during Korea. I'll confess that even then I thought you were officer material. Well, anyway, if you don't know a man well enough to call him by his first name after going through three weeks of hell with him at Ft. Benning, you never will.

"Oh, by the way, I want you to know that General Crinshaw wanted to be here today, but he had to keep a tennis appointment with General Kien."

Now Gerber really felt ill. Crinshaw was the kind of general who liked to do his own ass chewing. If he hadn't seen fit to come, Gerber must really be in deep kimchi.

"Mack," General Hull began again, "Alan here showed me that report of yours about using a motorboat for patrolling the river and ambushing the VC. I must say that it represents exactly the kind of unorthodox thinking that has made Special Forces so famous, or so infamous, depending upon your point of view. We understand that you acquired the boat through unofficial channels, after you tried to get one following standard procedures, but couldn't. We also understand that you no longer have the boat, which is probably a good thing. General Crinshaw has not seen the report and has no knowledge of it. He never will. After showing it to Admiral Speas and Lieutenant Commander Russell here, I destroyed it. From this moment on, I want it clearly understood that as far as the men in this room are concerned, the report, and the boat, never existed. Do you understand what I'm telling you?"

"Yes, General. Although I don't understand why," Gerber answered.

"To begin with, because I don't want to see the best damned A-detachment commander in Special Forces have his career go down the drain. Nor the best B-detachment commander, for that matter," said Hull, glancing meaningfully at Bates. "Also because we've got in mind a little operation that ought to be right up your team's alley. Since you'll be working directly with Russell here, I think I'll let him explain the concept to you."

Hull turned to Speas. "If that's all right with you, Admiral?"

"I'm just here to lend the Navy's official stamp of approval to this business, and offer my personal endorsement. Which means I'm here to make sure things don't blow up in the

Navy's face, or in mine. Go ahead, Dick, tell the man why he and you are here. He looks like he's about to die of curiosity."

"Thank you, Admiral."

"Lieutenant Gerber, uh, I mean Captain Gerber, I'm part of the Brown Water Navy. We run coastal patrols and interdict river traffic, something like you've been doing with that thing we were talking about that never existed.

"For the last couple of months, I've been attached to a division of Naval Advisory Group known as CODS, that's Combined Operations Developmental Study. My duties there have consisted mainly of the development of feasibility studies to determine the possibilities of joint operations between the Navy and the other services. As it happens, it seems that your AO is peculiarly suited to the type of operation envisioned by one of the studies we've been considering.

"As you know, Intelligence estimates have indicated a suspected major build-up of supplies by the Viet Cong in preparation for an early spring offensive. Estimated major VC staging areas for the offensive are thought to be in the Sa Dec and Go Cong areas and at Cho Moi. The last was confirmed in part by the interrogation of the prisoner captured by your team in Cai Thoi, and by intelligence gathered in Cho Moi itself by Sergeants Tran and Tri of your LLDB counterpart team. Certain information available to us indicates that Cho Moi is currently functioning as the major VC supply depot, but that shortly after Christmas the VC plan to shift the majority of supplies to Sa Dec and Go Cong, due to the limited facilities available to them at Cho Moi. A second build-up will then follow, with the VC shifting supplies from Cho Moi again as their distribution network is able to disperse them in the other areas. If we can hit the VC before they shift things out of Cho Moi in the next couple of weeks, we can really screw up their operation, cost them a lot of supplies, and postpone their offensive. As the field commander most familiar with that area, you would be the logical choice to lead such an operation, at least the American part of it.

"What we would like to do is make this thing into a joint Army-Navy-ARVN show. With that in mind, Lieutenant Colonel Bates and General Hull are arranging for the temporary transfer of two Tai strike companies to your command. We are also going to arrange to borrow a company of South Vietnamese Rangers, and an ARVN one-oh-five howitzer battery. In the interests of maintaining our advisory role, these will be placed under the temporary command of Lieutenant Minh, your counterpart at Camp A-five-five-five. Air support for the operation will be provided by U.S. Army helicopter gunships, and by fifth Aircommando Group."

Russell opened a briefcase and produced a map covered with an acetate overlay. It was a large-scale map of the area surrounding Cho Moi, but there was nothing marked on the map. He tapped the surface lightly with his fingertip.

"We have been able to confirm that the main base camp for the Cho Moi area lies in this area here, along the Kinh Ky Canal, and that it is defended by elements of the Viet Cong one-twenty-ninth Main Force Battalion. What we would like is for you and Lieutenant Minh to go in there with the two strike companies and the ARVN Ranger company that we will provide, as well as the two strike companies from your command, and clean things out for us. What do you say?"

Gerber was temporarily dumbfounded. This was not what he had expected at all.

"Well," he said, "first, I'd like to say I now understand why a Caribou dropped down out of the sky and unloaded three-and-a-half tons of C-rations at my camp this morning. Also I'd like to say that it seems to me we're talking about an awful lot of men in the field to have a captain running the show. Not that I'm complaining, you understand."

"We've fixed that," interrupted Bates. "Since the Navy seems to find our captain a little bit confusing with their captain, you're being administratively, temporarily, promoted to major. You'll revert back to captain on completion of the mission."

"Easy come, easy go," smiled Gerber. "The other thing I'd like to say is that I don't think it can be done. The ground in that area is like a peat bog. We might be able to move men through there on foot, but there's no decent place to put in an air assault, and if you try to set up heavy guns in there, you're going to lose them in about four feet of mud."

"Trust us, Captain," said Russell. "That's where the Navy comes in."

"Mind telling me how?" Gerber asked.

"It's simple, Captain. At least I hope it is. We're going to provide a flotilla of twenty armored landing craft to carry your men into the area. We're also going to provide an escort of six SWIFT boats and two PTGBs to provide direct fire support, as well as a command and communications boat, and a battalion aid boat. The one-oh-five battery is being mounted on floating platforms which will be anchored against the riverbank to provide indirect fire support."

Gerber was astounded. It seemed a preposterous plan, yet for the life of him, he couldn't see why it wouldn't work.

"Have you thought about the depth of the water you're going to be operating in?" he asked.

"The maximum draft of any of the vessels involved is five feet, four inches," Russell answered. "Most of them don't require anywhere near that."

Gerber was thoughtful for a moment, rubbing his chin.

"Well damn it man, do you want the job or not?" Speas snapped impatiently.

"I didn't realize I had a choice," answered Gerber. "Of course I want it. If I passed up an opportunity to do something as screwy as this, Fetterman and Kepler would never forgive me. Tell me, Admiral, does this Polish bar mitzvah have a name yet?"

"The Naval part of the mission is officially designated as Support Flotilla, Special Field Studies Force. SF-Cube for short."

Gerber groaned. "Can't the military name anything without making an acronym out of it?"

"Nope," replied Bates. "And you better come up with a good one because you get to figure out what we're going to call the Army part of it."

Gerber was quiet for a moment, then slowly began to chuckle. "All right, but you're going to be sorry, because I always wanted to do this. Suppose we call it Supported Force Leading Interdictory Strike."

Speas looked puzzled, but Bates, Hull, and Russell burst into laughter. Hull fairly howled.

"All right, Mack, I approve, although the Pentagon will probably change it, if anyone there is smart enough to figure it out. SFLIS it is."

"What about an overall operational name?" asked Russell.

"That one's already been decided," said Hull. "By me. We're going to call it River Raid."

Sergeant Taylor brought in the coffee, and the five officers spent the rest of the morning discussing details pertinent to the logistics and operational control of the mission. At 1130, Admiral Speas left for another meeting, and General Hull departed shortly thereafter. Bates had Taylor send out for lunch so that he, Gerber, and Russell could continue working out the myriad problems that kept cropping up.

Russell felt that Gerber should be aboard the C and C boat, so that the interface between the Naval support forces and the infantry command would be more effective.

Gerber felt that he should be ashore, leading his men.

Bates tended to sympathize with Gerber, but felt that it might be best if they were to arrange for a helicopter to serve as airborne C and C for the land-based phase of the operation. The concept had been tested before, and found to provide superior observation of both friendly and enemy troop movements, allowing the operational commander to respond quickly to changes in the developing battle by shifting his troops around to meet new threats or to outflank the enemy. The drawback was that Gerber would be unable to accompany the assault force to the landing area because the helicopter consumed fuel faster than the slow-moving armored troop carriers, towing the artillery, could get to the operational area. In order to solve that problem, it was decided to establish a Forward Operating Base for the Naval support unit closer to Gerber's camp.

That presented another whole set of problems to be dealt with. The terrain around Gerber's camp was not suitable for mooring large numbers of vessels, and it was known that local Viet Cong from the nearby village of Moc Phuc kept the camp under casual observation. Another area would have to be found which was near to both Cho Moi and the camp, had a good stretch of relatively clear river front, and was not likely to attract the attention of the Viet Cong. If such a location could be found, the flotilla would be moved into it a day or two before the raid, passing Cho Moi and the Kinh Ky Canal area under cover of darkness to avoid observation by the enemy. There they could be refueled from an armored landing craft that would accompany the riverine force as a floating tanker, and receive final preparation for the assault.

After some thought, Gerber finally said, "I've got just the place for you, Commander. It's got a long frontage on the river. It's about halfway between Cho Moi and my camp, and it's even got a fair-sized boat dock already there. Besides that, it's the last place the VC would ever think of looking for your men."

"Great," said Russell. "What's the name of this place?"

"It's called Ahn Tap."

Russell paled noticeably. He'd heard of the massacre.

"Come on, Mack, be serious," said Bates.

"I am serious, Colonel. Deadly so. Look, it's in the right area. It's got plenty of space and an existing dock, although I'll admit there are no facilities. It's one of the few places around there where we can get helicopters in and out safely. And it's absolutely the last place that Charlie would look for anything suspicious because he already knows that there's nothing there. You don't go looking for people in an area where you've just annihilated everybody. Russell can bring his people upriver after dark. I can have a pathfinding team at Ahn Tap to guide them in when they get to the area. They can lay over there the next day and evening, refueling and getting things lined up. Then we'll move downstream early the next morning, anchor the floating artillery at the mouth of the Kinh Ky Canal, and move on in and hit the Cong just after dawn, when they're still half asleep. That way we should have good visibility for the air cover as well."

Both men had to concede that the plan made good sense. The target date was set for three and a half weeks hence. Five days before Christmas.

By late afternoon, they had finished for the day, and Bates took them over to the Officer's Club for a drink, ordering Beam's Choice all around.

Gerber downed his in a single gulp. "Christ that's smooth."

Russell, doing his best to follow suit, tended to disagree. He wasn't really much of a drinker, he explained.

Gerber, however, suffered from no such qualms of conscience. He enjoyed a drink of good bourbon now and then. In fact, it was possible that he was enjoying a good drink of bourbon just a little too much too often of late, a fact that hadn't really escaped his own attention. He'd simply made a conscious decision to ignore it. He'd discovered that as long as he was busy with the duties of his job, he didn't have time to think about Karen. When he wasn't busy, he'd discovered that he didn't have to think about her at all, provided that he could keep his brain cells comfortably numb. He ordered another drink for Bates and Russell, and two more for himself, making his own doubles.

"You seem to have a powerful thirst tonight, Mack," Bates observed dryly.

Gerber laughed it off. "You know how it is, Colonel. Drink 'em if ya got 'em. This stuff is kind of hard to come by out in the field."

"Sure."

Bates watched, nursing his own drink, as Gerber drained his doubles, then signaled the bartender for another. When it arrived, Bates said, "Why don't we order an early dinner and get down to some serious drinking?"

Russell apologized, saying he had made other plans for dinner, but would be sure to speak to both of them in the morning about any further considerations relating to the planned operation. Then he made his exit, as Bates had hoped he might. As soon as the Naval officer had gone, Bates turned to Gerber.

"Okay, Mack, I assume that things did not go well between you and the young lady in Nha Trang. You want to tell me about it?"

"I don't know what you mean, Colonel," said Gerber innocently. He noticed with a sense of abstract detachment that he had slurred over the word colonel slightly. The booze was beginning to hit him.

"Come on, Mack, you don't have to play cute with me. I can see right through you like a piece of rice paper. I'm the guy who sent you up there to fix things up between the two of you, remember?"

"Well," said Gerber, "it didn't work."

"So what went wrong?" Bates pressed.

"Hell, I don't know, Alan. One minute everything was fine, and the next minute she was telling me to forget it ever happened." Gerber realized it was the first time he'd ever called Bates by his first name.

"You say something to piss her off?"

"I don't think so. I tried to get her to talk to me about it, and she went away in a huff."

"I figured something was amiss when you came back from R and R a day early," Bates told him.

"It's amiss all right, but I don't know what it is," said Gerber. "I figured that was the last I was ever going to hear from her, but I've had two letters since."

"Well," mused Bates, "at least she's talking to you."

"I'm not sure if she's talking to me or past me. The first letter didn't say a thing about the blow-up. It was just one of those 'Hi! How are you? I'm fine' kind of letters. Telling me what she'd been doing lately, that kind of thing. She didn't mention our fight at all. Hell, I don't even know if you can call it a fight or not. I stood there and she kicked me. It seemed awfully final at the time."

"Weird," agreed Bates.

"So anyway, I wrote her back. Told her I still loved her, was sorry for whatever it was I'd done wrong, and wanted to see her again."

"Sounds like a good move so far."

"And do you know what happens?" Gerber continued. "Today, just before I get on the plane to come here, the mail pouch arrives with a letter from her, and do you know what she says?"

Bates realized it was a rhetorical question, but he was supposed to say something. "No. What?"

"First she says she doesn't want a serious relationship right now. Then she says she thinks, however, that I'm the kind of person she'd like to have a serious relationship with, someday. Then comes the real kicker. She says that since it isn't fair to ask me to wait, she thinks it would be best if we didn't see each other again, although she'd still like me to write to her for Christ's sake. She also tells me she's being TDY'd to Hue, which for practical purposes might as well be Seattle, or someplace equally remote, like the dark side of the moon, and then signs the damned letter 'Love Kari'. Now you tell me, what am I supposed to make of that shit?"

"Christ!" said Bates. "No wonder you drink. Looks to me like you made a bad mistake with this woman."

"Looks to me like we both made a mistake. She made the mistake of telling me that she loved me. And I made the mistake of believing her."

"In that case, I think we'd better go downtown," said Bates.

Gerber looked properly shocked. "Colonel, if you're about to suggest we go visit one of the kind of houses I think you're about to suggest we go visit, I think you ought to know that I'm feeling pretty asexual right now."

"I was about to suggest nothing of the sort," said Bates. "Although all things considered, that might well be the best thing you could do right now, provided you didn't catch yourself fifteen of the ten known social diseases in the process. What I was going to suggest, and didn't think we ought to do here in the club, since this is where you met the lady, if I remember correctly… What I was going to suggest, was that it seems to me that in a case like this, there's only one thing left to do."

"What's that?" said Gerber.

"Get drunk. Come on. I'll get Taylor's jeep and we'll drive downtown."

"Thanks, Colonel," said Gerber. "But you know what? The thing to do isn't to get drunk. It's to get very drunk."

They did.

CHAPTER 15

SPECIAL FORCES CAMP A-555

Fetterman was not amused.

He'd just found out from Bromhead that Le Quan Kim was leaving in the morning. The powers that be had finally figured out what to do with the twice-orphaned boy. What they had figured out to do with him was to send him in an orphanage down in Can Tho. It made sense, they reasoned. The boy was an orphan, so he belonged in an orphanage. Fetterman thought it sucked. It was ten days before Christmas, and to Fetterman's way of thinking, nobody ought to have to spend Christmas in an orphanage. It was an area where he could speak from personal experience.

The boy should have been removed from the camp weeks ago, Fetterman knew, but it hadn't worked out that way, which was fine with both of them. To begin with, nobody had been exactly sure what to do with Le. For a few days he'd been kind of a curiosity as the sole survivor of the Ahn Tap massacre. Kepler and Tran had questioned him at length over a three day period, trying to drag out any little scrap of information the boy might have buried away in his memory of that awful night. Hopefully, something might prove helpful in tracking down those responsible. In the end, the only noteworthy piece of information they'd extracted was the knowledge that the large Viet Cong raiding force that attacked Ahn Tap was advised by a Chinese officer.

"One of these days, buddy, you and I are going to meet face to face," Fetterman promised himself. "And when we do, you aren't going to like it much."

After the initial novelty had worn off, it had been fairly easy for Le to get sort of misplaced. There were a lot of civilians wandering around the camp, families of strikers, and one more boy was easily overlooked. Especially a small, timid sort of boy. Once or twice Gerber had thought to inquire after the boy's wellbeing. On those occasions a word or two on Fetterman's part with McMillan had generated the Doc's considered and profound medical opinion that it would not be in the boy's best interests to remove him completely from familiar surroundings so soon after a traumatic experience. It was a bunch of bull, and Gerber knew it, but he let it slide. He had enough problems of his own to deal with.

So the boy had stayed in camp, and Fetterman had spent more and more of his free time with him, teaching him by demonstration and pantomime example how to do the things he'd considered important as a kid: sharpen a knife properly, make a bow and arrow, fold a paper airplane, whittle a whistle.

He'd learned from Le on that one. Fetterman had carved the whistle, and when he'd finished it, Le had reciprocated by making a flute out of bamboo which he gave to the master sergeant. Fetterman's attempts at playing it had almost gotten him ejected from the camp by the other A-team members.

And now they were going to ship the kid off to an orphanage. It just wasn't fair. Fetterman decided he was going to do something about it. He was going to have a talk with Gerber.

Gerber wasn't in his hootch, so the master sergeant went looking for him. First he tried the commo bunker. The commanding officer wasn't there. Neither, he noticed, was

Schmidt. Bocker was standing radio watch. It seemed to Fetterman that Bocker was perpetually standing radio watch.

"Where's the new guy?" Fetterman asked.

"Schmidt?" said Bocker, looking up from a dogeared copy of *Popular Electronics*. "He likes the night shift. He's catching some zees right now."

"Where?"

"Isn't he in his hammock?" Bocker glanced around. "That's odd. I could have sworn he was in it just a minute ago. Maybe I didn't notice him go out."

"Maybe. You got any idea where the Captain is?"

"I think I saw him earlier over by the team bunker."

"Thanks."

Fetterman walked across the compound, his boots kicking up little puffs of the dirty red dust that seemed to cover all of Vietnam. He found Gerber inside the team bunker, getting a cup of coffee. As he came down the steps, Gerber took a sip, and swore.

"Goddamnit! What the hell is wrong with this coffeepot?"

Anderson looked up from the corner where he was artfully sketching a Christmas tree on the wall with a piece of green chalk. "It was working fine, earlier, Captain. Here, let me have a look."

Anderson came over to inspect the pot.

"Plug's loose, that's all," he said, fiddling with the socket. He bent the prongs out a bit more so they would hold tighter, stuck the plug back in, and wiggled it slightly to make sure it fit tight. The coffee pot started making gurgling sounds.

"That should do it, sir. It'll take a couple of minutes to get hot again."

"Captain, is this a bad time, or can I speak with you for a minute?" Fetterman interrupted.

"Come on in, Sergeant. I'd offer you a cup of coffee, but it's cold as usual."

Anderson took the hint and said, "I'll be back in a few minutes. Got to find some white chalk for the star on top." He walked out, apparently oblivious to the piece of white chalk sticking out of his breast pocket.

"What is it, Tony?" said Gerber when Anderson was gone.

"Sir, it's about the boy, Le Quan Kim. Do we have to send him down to that orphanage in Can Tho?"

Gerber sat down at the table and motioned Fetterman to take a chair opposite him.

"I'm afraid so, Tony. That's the decision from the Civil Affairs people in Saigon. Besides, we've got to do something with him. We can't just leave him wandering around the camp."

"Why not sir? What's one more civilian, more or less? The camp's full of them."

"Those are families of the strikers, Tony. You know why they're here. They wouldn't be safe anyplace else. Not with their husbands fighting for us. Anyway, who would take care of him?"

"Me sir. I'll look after the little guy."

"You, Master Sergeant? And what about when you're out on patrol?"

"I'll get one of the other guys to keep an eye on him. We're practically never all out at once, sir. Besides, he's pretty independent. He doesn't take much looking after. He can almost take care of himself."

Gerber thought he could see where this was leading, and thought it would be best to head it off before it got too far gone.

"All right, Master Sergeant," he said sternly. "Suppose you tell me just who is going to look after him when you're gone. Who's going to keep an eye on the little guy when you're rotated back to The World."

Fetterman's answer surprised him.

"You're right sir. That wouldn't do at all. Would you be kind enough to have Lieutenant Colonel Bates inquire in Saigon about the proper method of commencing adoption proceedings?"

"Whoa, wait a minute now, Tony. Don't you think this is all a bit sudden? Hadn't you better talk this over with Mrs. Fetterman and the kids, first?"

"I can assure you that won't be a problem, sir. If you'll have Lieutenant Colonel Bates get the ball rolling, I'll write to Mrs. Fetterman and the kids."

"This is a pretty big decision you're making here. Are you sure you've thought this thing through?"

"Yes sir, I have, and I want to adopt the boy."

"And how about the boy? Does he want to be adopted? By you?"

"I haven't been able to discuss it with him yet, sir. As you know, Vietnamese is one of the few languages I don't speak. As soon as I leave, I'm going to get Lieutenant Minh and have him interpret for me."

"This kid really got to you, didn't he?" asked Gerber. "What is it about him that makes you so sure you're doing the right thing?"

Fetterman shrugged. "I don't know sir. I guess it's because he's a natural-born survivor. I can feel that kind of thing about a person. I look at him, and I see the kid that was me thirty years ago. He deserves a better life than this country's got to offer him, especially in an orphanage. I want to help him out if I can."

"But are you sure this is the best way to do it? You're talking about making him your son. Have you considered what life would be like for him in America, where everything is strange and the people are different? They won't speak his language, or have the same customs or value system. Hell Tony, the boy doesn't even know what a flush toilet is."

"He can learn, sir."

"Can he learn to deal with racial prejudice as well? That's going to be a real problem in the States, and you know it."

"Captain, Vietnam isn't exactly free of racial prejudice either you know. He gets along well with me, and he gets along well enough with the Tais, and you know how they feel about most Vietnamese. The way they look at it, the Vietnamese stole their country from them, just like we did to the American Indian. I'm telling you the boy will adapt. He's a survivor. In America at least he'll have a chance to grow old enough to find out what racial prejudice is all about. That's more than he'll have here."

"Your mind seems to be firmly made up on this subject, Master Sergeant."

"Yes sir. It is."

"*Chieu hoi*, Master Sergeant, *chieu hoi*. I give up. I'll speak to Colonel Bates and see what we can do. That's all I'm promising. I have a hunch that Vietnamese red tape is going to make the American bureaucracy look like a smooth, well-organized, well-oiled machine."

"Thank you sir. In the meantime, is it okay if the boy stays here?"

"Ah, hah, now we come to the meat of the problem. You don't want the boy to have to spend Christmas in that orphanage, is that it?"

"Yes sir. Something like that, sir."

"Well," sighed Gerber, "I suppose it might be possible that there won't be space available for him on the helicopter in the morning. Maybe you should have another talk with Doc McMillan. I'll bet Le is developing a high fever even as we speak."

"You know about my little talks with the Doc, sir?"

Gerber just smiled. "I do want you to realize one thing, Tony. The petition for adoption might not be approved. Even if it is, it could take months. We can't go on hiding the boy forever, especially since they already know we've got him. Sooner or later, he's going to have to go to Can Tho, and when that time comes, I don't expect an argument, understood?"

"Understood, sir. And thank you."

"No problem. Now don't you think you'd better find Minh and go have that talk with the boy?"

"Yes sir. I'll go do that right now, sir."

"Tony, there's one more thing. I kind of hate to have to say this, but the extra troops are going to start arriving later this afternoon, and we're going to be pretty busy after that. Part of them are from Kevin Petersen's strike force, so they should be okay, but we're going to have to check the rest of them out. That means arms inspection for everybody, and range instruction starting first thing tomorrow morning. I want to make sure that when these people start shooting, they shoot at the Viet Cong, not us."

"Understood sir. I'll arrange to be available from thirteen hundred hours on. Shall I tell Sergeant Tyme as well?"

"Affirmative. But tell him fourteen hundred ought to be soon enough."

"Yes sir. Will there be anything else?"

"Only that you don't have to call me sir when it's just the two of us. I've told you that before."

"Yes sir," Fetterman answered with a smile. "I know that, sir." He turned and went up the bunker stairs.

Gerber sat for a moment shaking his head. He was convinced that he had the best damned team sergeant in Special Forces, yet the man never ceased to surprise him. He was a walking contradiction, physically, mentally, and now it seemed, emotionally.

Gerber got up and walked over to the coffeepot. He poured himself a cup, and tasted it cautiously.

It was like biting into a snowball.

The first of the reinforcements came in at about 1430 that afternoon aboard a couple of C-130 Hercules. The big transport planes ate up disconcerting amounts of runway during landing, but had no difficulty taking off after discharging their troops.

Lieutenant Bao's Tais had been vigorously patrolling the area around the camp for two days in the interest of keeping it clear of Viet Cong. While it was possible that a dedicated VC observer might sneak through for a look at the camp, the patrol greatly diminished the likelihood that he would be able to get back out with any truly interesting information. It had also produced the unexpected side benefit of terminating the harassing rocket and mortar fire the camp was accustomed to receiving on an irregular but frequent basis, and made the ground fire situation much more pleasant for the pilots.

Bao and Hung had a bit of difficulty getting the reinforcements organized until they turned the task over to Sergeant Krung. By 1530 hours, Fetterman and Tyme were conducting a basic review of the use, function, and maintenance of individual weapons to an attentive company of Tai strikers under the watchful scowl of the wiry tribesman. If any of them seemed to be losing interest in the proceedings, a mere frown from Krung was sufficient to insure enthusiastic attendance to the remainder of the lecture.

While that was going on, Gerber, Bromhead, and Kepler were in closed conference with Lieutenant Commander Russell, who had flown out to the camp with his executive officer, Lieutenant Spike Patterson, in order to discuss final details of the deployment and get a first-hand look at the dock and frontage available at Ahn Tap. Both men had evaluated the primitive facilities as adequate for the purpose, once they had gotten over the initial shock of seeing the destruction of the place.

It was agreed that a patrol from Camp A-555 would be inserted into the area around Ahn Tap by helicopter on the morning of the seventeenth of December. The patrol would make a reconnaissance of the area, looking for any sign of recent visitation by the Viet Cong. If nothing was found, they would signal the camp by radio, and the message would be relayed to Russell, who would be standing by with the river task force in Saigon. The vessels would then proceed upriver, traveling under cover of darkness, and with such speed as would be required to reach Ahn Tap on the night of the eighteenth.

The Special Forces patrol in Ahn Tap would assist them in locating and maneuvering into their anchorage at Ahn Tap by means of radio and handheld strobe lights. The boats would refuel and take care of such field maintenance as might be necessary during the day of the nineteenth, at which time the assault troops would be brought in by helicopter from Gerber's camp.

The flotilla would set out for Cho Moi at 0430 hours, arrive in the AO just after dawn, establish a floating fire base for the howitzer battery, and then proceed to attack the VC supply cache located along the bank of the Kinh Ky Canal. One company of Tais would move overland to form a blocking force, while the other three companies and the Rangers made the assault from ATCs that would maneuver up the canal.

The SWIFT boats and PTGBs would provide direct fire support for the assaulting element, and ensure the control of the river and any canals which might be used as avenues of escape by the Viet Cong.

They were just about to break anyway, and have one of the beers the Navy men had brought in with them, when Fetterman and Bocker appeared at the entryway of the team bunker.

"Captain, may we see you outside for a moment?" Fetterman seemed unnaturally serious.

Gerber excused himself from the meeting and went outside.

"Okay guys, what's up?"

Bocker looked hopefully at Fetterman, who nodded, then spoke.

"Sergeant Bocker just received a message for you from Saigon, sir. Lieutenant Karen Morrow was aboard an aircraft that developed engine trouble over the Highlands. They went down just outside Dak To. There's no word on any survivors. Lieutenant Colonel Bates thought you'd want to know."

Gerber thought for a minute that he was going to pass out, then his knees steadied under him, and he nodded.

"Thank you, Master Sergeant," he said, fully aware of the break in his voice. "Sergeant Bocker, would you please work some of your electronic wizardry and see if you can get a hold of Captain Dave Henderson for me. I understand he's running an A-camp out of Dak To now."

Without another word, Gerber turned and went back to his meeting.

CHAPTER 16

THE VILLAGE OF AHN TAP

Fetterman sat in the back of the UH-1D Huey slick, feeling the sweat drip off his forehead and onto his tiger-striped jungle fatigues. In his stomach there was that old familiar feeling of butterflies, but his hands were steady. As always, except for the butterflies, he felt strangely calm.

His custom-tailored, many-pocketed fatigues were stuffed full of grenades, flares, combat dressings, and spare magazines for the suppressed Swedish-K submachine gun he held in his hands. The light, aluminum-framed nylon pack on his back and his web gear were filled with more of the same, five days' worth of rations, and a tiny but brilliant SDU-5E xenon strobe marker light. Strapped to the top of the pack was a heavy, powerful, night vision scope, one of the new passive Starlight models that had recently arrived at the camp, along with fresh batteries for the existing IR weapons sights. A pair of 7X50mm binoculars hung around his neck.

On the opposite side of the canvas bench seat, Sully Smith sat chewing gum, and smiling as if someone had just told him the world's dirtiest joke. The only time he forgot to smile was when he accidentally glanced across the cargo compartment and his eyes fell on Schmidt.

Clearly, Schmidt was not happy about being there. He looked even more sickly and emaciated than usual, his skin seeming positively bleached. He had turned up his collar, covered the lower half of his face with a black bandana, and pulled his black boonie hat down around his ears, and then wrapped himself, radio, machine gun, and all, tightly in his poncho-liner blanket. He huddled against the transmission housing, shivering as if he were having a malaria attack.

Smith frowned as he looked at Schmidt. He knew the FNG wasn't a coward. He'd proved that in Cai Thoi, when he'd captured the VC and killed the other three as easily as if he'd been filleting a fish for breakfast, and with no more emotion. Yet here he was, shaking like a man with the palsy, and huddled beneath his blanket as though trying to avoid the rising sunlight at all costs. At least he'd come out in the sunlight, which made Smith feel a little better, but not much.

The rest of the helicopter was filled with three heavily armed Tais, LLDB Sergeant Xuyen, who had the other radio, and Doc McMillan, who sat absently fiddling with an M-79 grenade launcher, the stem of an unlit briar pipe clenched tightly between his teeth.

The helicopter came in fast over a low paddy dike, and touched down briefly in high grass near a treeline. The men leaped out and sprinted into the trees as the Huey clattered back into the sky again. It was the third time that morning that the helicopter had landed. It would make two more landings a couple of miles away. The idea was to confuse any VC in the area as to exactly where the recon team had been inserted.

The men established a defensive circle in a thicket, feet touching, and waited for nearly half an hour until they could be reasonably certain that their landing had not been observed by anyone in the immediate vicinity. Then they moved quickly in the direction of Ahn Tap.

Near the outskirts, they found a good spot in a small stand of bamboo, and established a day laager, where they could rest and take turns observing the ruined village. It was a nightmare landscape of blackened, tumbled-down huts and charred corrals that had once held pigs, goats, and water buffalo alongside pens of ducks and chickens. All of it was now devoid of life and gone to ash. Near the edge of the town, the shattered remains of the schoolhouse lay in heaped-up piles of rubble; an occasional stray brick or twisted steel chair scattered haphazardly about, the dead teacher's massive desk was unmoved, albeit already rusting. In the front yard of the school, a shiny new bell, the replacement for the one thrown into the river, stood in silent mockery to the destruction, safe in its brick cupola. Only the bell, and the long wooden dock, barely visible from this location, remained intact.

Fearing that Schmidt was coming down with something serious, Fetterman ordered him to rest while the others watched for any sign of movement. Although McMillan checked the commo sergeant's condition frequently, he was at a loss for any explanation. Schmidt's temperature was well below normal, and his blood pressure approached hypotension. He complained of chills, and his skin was cold and clammy. Treatment for heat exhaustion failed to produce any significant results. He was clearly photophobic. Finally, fearing that Schmidt was about to go into shock, McMillan administered adrenalin and Ringer's lactate, which only seemed to worsen his condition.

Schmidt continued to deteriorate throughout the day, causing Fetterman much concern. He knew that a medevac call could get Schmidt hospital attention within a matter of thirty minutes to an hour, but that it would also surely give away their position to any VC in the area, and cause them to wonder what the patrol was doing there.

Reluctantly, Fetterman decided that unless Schmidt's condition declined drastically, he would put off making his decision until after they had reconnoitered the village proper.

Then, should it be necessary, there was a chance that a helicopter might be able to come in and take him out unobserved. In the poorer lighting conditions near dusk, there was a possibility that even if the helicopter were observed, the team might successfully escape detection and be able to remain behind.

Shortly before noon, Fetterman sent Smith, Xuyen, and two of the Tais to make a broad sweep around the village, looking for signs that the VC might have been in the area. They returned at about 1500 hours and reported that they had found nothing except a single bare footprint and some deer tracks, both several days old.

"All right," said Fetterman. "Schmidt's still the same. Xuyen, Smith, you come with me. Let's go in and have a look at this place."

Fetterman wanted Xuyen with him because he was carrying the team's other radio. Smith, a demolitions specialist, had a penchant for locating booby traps. He was fond of saying that in order to know where to find booby traps, you first had to know where to hide them.

They moved into the village with great caution, leapfrogging ahead of one another so that the man advancing was always covered by the other two. They needn't have bothered. Even the buzzards had abandoned Ahn Tap.

Smith's search for booby traps was more fruitful. The only items of any interest left in the town were the docks, the school bell, the teacher's desk, and the town well. Smith checked them and found one booby trap at each location.

They were all crude devices employing simple pull wires attached to stick grenades, except for the one at the dock, which utilized a loose plank as a pressure plate with a block of

TNT underneath. All of them already showed signs of rust and weathering, which Smith pointed out to Fetterman.

"My guess is that they were left behind by the raiding party almost as an afterthought. There's nothing new around here. Pretty sloppy of the clean-up crew to have missed them, though. Lucky nobody got hurt."

"Maybe they looked too hard, and in all the wrong places," offered Fetterman.

"More than likely they didn't look at all," Smith said disgustedly. "Probably figured there wasn't anything left worth booby trapping. Still, you'd have thought some schmuck would have tripped over this loose board. Or gotten thirsty and cranked himself up a bucketful of hurt."

"You're sure they're all old? The VC haven't been around here lately?"

Smith shrugged. "Who can tell where the VC are until they start shooting? Christ, Fetterman, I can't even tell who they are unless I see one aiming a rifle at my head. I am sure that these traps are all at least two, probably three weeks old, and possibly more. I can't say for certain if they were put here before or after the burial detail was here. All I can tell you is that they weren't set recently, they weren't done by an expert, and I haven't seen anything else."

"Okay. Let's get back to the others. We'll watch the ville for a while tonight, and if we don't see anything, we'll call camp and let the captain know the show is on."

When they reached the bamboo thicket, Fetterman was amazed to find Schmidt sitting up. He still looked awful, but then he always looked awful. He'd rigged his blanket cape over him in a sort of lean-to fashion, and seemed to be doing something with the insides of his radio.

"What's the story on Schmidt?" Fetterman asked, taking McMillan aside. "When we left, I thought he was at death's door."

"Damnedest thing I ever saw," McMillan answered in a low tone. "He just kept slipping away from me until he was pretty near comatose. I was almost sure it was shock of some kind, but he just wasn't responding to treatment. So I tried the only thing left."

"Which was?"

"I gave him two units of plasma, IV."

Fetterman arched an eyebrow.

Smith, who had been crouching nearby listening, shuddered involuntarily. "I told you that guy ain't human."

"Don't be ridiculous, Sully," snapped Fetterman.

"Oh, he's human all right," interjected McMillan. "At least I think he is. Physically speaking, he seems to have everything in the right place. His vital stats are a bit skewed, but you expect that, given his condition. In fact, I'm surprised at the speed of his recovery. Plasma is an old, established treatment for severe shock, but I've never seen it work this fast, and don't know what brought the shock on in the first place. It didn't quite fit the characteristics of heat exhaustion, and definitely wasn't sunstroke.

"I examined him for evidence of spider or snake bite, but couldn't find any puncture. He does seem to have a mild sunburn, though, which is a bit puzzling, considering the lengths he goes to, to avoid sunlight.

"It's his mental state I'm worried about. This avoidance of sunlight thing. The whole bit with the dark glasses. And his apparent lack of emotion. His performance at Cai Thoi as described by Derek and Sully."

"I thought his performance at Cai Thoi showed outstanding professionalism, and a damned cool head for somebody new to combat," Fetterman growled.

"Exactly. That's my point. It wasn't what you'd expect of a new man at all. It was too cool. A new man isn't supposed to kill with that kind of cold-bloodedness. It takes a while for combat to blunt the conditioned sensibilities society has imposed on us since we came out of the caves. Maybe you would have done it that way, Master Sergeant, but a new guy shouldn't have. I don't even think Smith here, would have. I've seen a lot of death and suffering, and I know I haven't become that hardened to it yet."

"Are you analyzing Schmidt or me?"

"I'm not analyzing anybody, Fetterman. I don't have the proper academic credentials nor the respect for Freud to do so. But I do think that Schmidt's behavior could be indicative of some deeper, repressed personality disorder. I think maybe when this thing is over, we ought to send him to Saigon to see a psychiatrist."

"Bah! A man does his job well, and you want to make him into a nut case."

"Fetterman," said McMillan, "I was in Cai Thoi with Sergeant Tam on a medcap two days after Smith, Kepler, and Schmidt were there. The villagers were terrified. When we asked why, they didn't want to talk about it at first, but finally one of them told us it was because of the vampire. He showed us the bodies. They were still in the hut. The villagers were afraid to touch them. After two days they were pretty badly deteriorated. You know what the heat here can do to a corpse. Tam and I didn't mention the incident, because we didn't want to fuel the paranoia already floating around camp, but we both agreed in our findings. In each case, death was caused by blood loss, resulting from two puncture wounds to the carotid artery, here in the neck, caused by some small, sharp-pointed object resembling an ice pick."

"Christ!" snorted Fetterman. "Talk about paranoia. Now you're telling me the guy really *is* a vampire."

"I'm telling you I believe he thinks he is. For practical purposes, there may not be much difference."

CHAPTER 17

C AND C BOAT, SF^3, BEN TAU WHARF, SAIGON

"All right, gentlemen, let's have some quiet in here," said Russell. "Hooper, turn off that damned radio, will you?"

"But Commander Russell, it's the Stones. You can't just turn off the Stones like that."

"Lieutenant Hooper, and for the moment you are still a lieutenant, this is an operational briefing, not a beach party. Turn that thing off. Now."

Hooper reluctantly switched off the radio.

"I'm sorry about this, Major," Russell said to Gerber. "The Brown Water Navy's always been kind of a loose outfit, and I'm afraid Hooper is a bit looser than the rest of us. Sometimes I think his brain is loose."

Gerber smiled indulgently, and waited for Russell to get things organized. The men crowded into the small armored command post aboard the converted LCM looked more like a group of college freshmen at their first kegger than experienced seamen and fighters. Some were dressed in khakis or fatigues, while others wore navy denims. One was even attired in a pair of cut-off shorts and a skivvy shirt. Only Russell wore a complete uniform of tropical whites. Even Gerber, used to the informal dress code of his Special Forces camp, was a bit surprised at the apparent laxity of discipline.

Russell began. "This will be the final briefing before sailing orders are issued. Major Gerber and Sergeant Kepler have to get back to their base, so they'll run through their part of the show and give us the latest update on local intelligence. Let's give them our attention so they can get on their way before they lose the light."

Russell turned to Gerber. "Major, it's your show."

Gerber still wasn't used to being addressed as "Major." It took him half a second to realize Russell meant him.

"I think, Commander, that it might work out better to let Sergeant Kepler go first. Are you ready, Sergeant?"

"Yes sir." He addressed Russell. "Has a guard been posted, sir?"

"A guard?"

"Yes sir. Today's briefing is classified as 'Secret,' sir."

"Sergeant, we're on a boat floating in the middle of the Saigon River. There aren't any spies here."

"With respect, sir, we are not floating in the middle of the river. We are tied up to the dock. It is procedure, sir."

Russell shrugged. "Chief, see to it, will you?"

The chief petty officer, a white-haired, beefy-looking guy in dungarees, disappeared. A few moments later he came back in and closed the hatch behind him.

"Gunner's mate Hess is outside with a forty-five, sir."

Russell nodded, and Kepler resumed his talk, uncovering the map board.

"Gentlemen, today's briefing is classified 'Secret,' and is not to be discussed," he cautioned again.

"This is the operational area. The Kinh Ky Canal just north of Cho Moi. For some weeks now, intelligence reports have indicated a major build-up of arms and supplies in this area by the Viet Cong. Our job is to go in there and neutralize it. The main VC base is believed to be located in this area here, on the east bank of the canal itself.

"Although the precise location of the enemy encampment is not known, we have good evidence suggesting that our estimates are accurate. There has been a large amount of sampan and river-junk traffic in the area, and the one-twenty-ninth Main Force Battalion of the Viet Cong are known to be guarding the supply cache. Members of the one-twenty-ninth have been observed on several occasions in the town of Cho Moi itself.

"Upon receipt of confirmation, which should arrive later tonight, your flotilla will proceed to My Tho in the delta area of the Mekong. You will lay over there tomorrow, and then proceed immediately afterward to here." He changed maps. "The former village of Ahn Tap. Movement is being made under cover of darkness to avoid observation by the enemy.

"You will be met at Ahn Tap by a pathfinder team, which will guide you into an anchorage there. You must be in position by dawn on the nineteenth. From that point on, any and all river traffic is to be considered suspect, and stopped and detained.

"Reports from our team in Ahn Tap indicate that so far, there is no sign of any VC observers in the area. We want to keep it that way.

"Beginning about fifteen hundred hours on the nineteenth, four companies of troops will be brought into Ahn Tap by helicopter from Special Forces Camp A-five-five-five, located north of the area, here. We're bringing the troops in during the late afternoon to minimize the hazards of an accident occurring after dusk, and to give them a chance to eat and rest before embarkation.

"At precisely oh-four-thirty hours on the morning of the twentieth, you will embark the troops aboard ATCs for the target area, and proceed to this area here."

Kepler switched back to the original map.

"At this point here, you will establish an anchorage for the one-oh-five mm howitzer battery that will accompany you in tow when you leave Saigon. The howitzers will provide indirect fire support for the landing and subsequent operation.

"At oh-five-thirty, a fifth company of troops will be inserted by helicopter at this point here, just outside Cho Moi itself, and proceed on foot across this marshy area to take up positions here and here as a blocking force.

"At exactly oh-six-thirty, the howitzer battery will prep the landing area, and at oh-six-forty the first company will go ashore here, the second here. They will be followed ten minutes later by the third company, and two platoons of the fourth. The remainder of the fourth company will remain aboard ship, and will orbit here, at the mouth of the canal, as a ready reserve and reaction force.

"Once landed, the troops will proceed inland, close with, and engage the enemy. Direct support for the landing will be handled by the flotilla's SWIFT boats and two PT gunboats, and by Army Aviation helicopter gunships. The gunships will support the troops after the landing. As mentioned, the VC stronghold is being defended by the one-twenty-ninth Main Force Battalion, which is made up of some of the best that Charlie has to offer in the region. I think we can expect a determined resistance. I also think that the ATCs and supporting gunships can anticipate a fair amount of automatic weapons and RPG fire. We are assuming that Charlie won't be expecting an operation of this sort, and probably feels protected, not threatened, by the canal, but experience has taught us that we can expect him to have well prepared positions covering all avenues of approach.

"Once the operation has been completed, and the enemy neutralized, his supplies destroyed, the troops will be reembarked aboard the ATCs for return to Ahn Tap, where they will again be picked up by helicopter and conveyed back to camp.

"Are there any questions?"

One of the men held up his hand.

"Yes Mister Roberts, what is it?" said Russell.

"I don't mean to sound obtuse or anything, especially this late in the game, but wouldn't it have been a whole lot simpler to just put those people in there by helicopter? All this shuffling back and forth from the camp to Ahn Tap to the canal and back again just seems a bit much."

"It would be simpler," said Kepler, "but it wouldn't be very effective. The only decent place to land a sizable force is where the blocking company is going in. The rest of the area is far too swampy. By the time we put all five companies into that area, and maneuvered them into position, Charlie would be long gone. We want to get the one-twenty-ninth as well as the supplies.

"Any further questions?"

"Yes," said a lieutenant junior grade, with a large chest, whose nametag said Gomoll. "I assume consideration has been given to how deep the water is in there, but just how wide is this canal? It doesn't look to me like there's much room to maneuver in there."

"There isn't. The width varies, but the average is ninety to one hundred yards."

Hooper let out a low whistle. "That is tight."

"Anyone else?"

There were no further questions, and Kepler turned things back over to Gerber.

"I really don't have anything to add. As usual, Sergeant Kepler has been most thorough with his briefing. I'm sure you gentlemen will have specific details to discuss among yourselves pertaining to your individual parts in the operation, and the Sergeant and I need to get back to camp. It's likely that I'll see some of you again in Ahn Tap. Until then, and if I don't, good luck."

The meeting continued for another hour after Gerber and Kepler left for Tan Son Nhut to catch their flight back to camp. Lieutenants junior grade Gomoll, Roberts, and Patterson would each command one two-boat section of the SWIFTs. Lieutenant Hooper, aboard the lead PTGB, would be in overall command of supporting forces. Russell would be in direct control of the landings aboard the C and C boat with the communications gear and new counter mortar radar. Each of the individual ATCs would be coxswained by a senior seaman under the command of a bosun.

When every contingency had been planned for that could be planned for, and the boats had all been fueled and made ready to sail on short notice, Russell wrote a long letter to his wife. He then paced about the command center until he made the radioman on watch nervous. Finally, he went topside.

It was a pleasant evening, and he was enjoying watching the lights of the city and the late evening traffic along Trinh Minh The Street and the Quay Bridge when the radio operator came up on deck.

"Message from Major Gerber, sir. He reports that there is no sign of enemy activity in Ahn Tap. The mission is on."

"Very good radioman. Signal the other boats to make preparation for getting underway. It's time we gave Charlie his early Christmas present."

CHAPTER 18

AHN TAP FORWARD OPERATING BASE

Schmidt had been sick again, during the day. Not as sick as yesterday, but still unable to do much. He'd been fine last night though, and McMillan had no explanation for the sudden relapse, other than a psychosomatic condition. Fetterman was almost willing to accept the Doc's notion. Shortly after sundown, Schmidt had made another recovery. He was up now and keeping an eye on the village with that incredible eyesight of his. Twice he'd picked up movement that Fetterman had only been able to confirm through the starlight scope. Both times it had turned out to be animals. Once it was a deer that had wandered along the edge of the village to drink from the river, the other time a wild tapir had come in from the jungle, rooted around a bit, and finding nothing of interest, ambled back out.

Fetterman had moved his patrol into the village after dusk, and established defensive positions near the dock area. They had held the village under constant observation for two days and nights without seeing another living soul. If everything was proceeding according to plan, and Fetterman had no reason to believe it was not, he knew that the riverine task force would by now have left My Tho and be cruising up river toward them. If there were no complications, the flotilla should arrive in Ahn Tap shortly after 0400. Until then, there was nothing to do but watch and wait.

Fetterman realized he was hungry. He rummaged in his pack until he found a C-ration. Unable to read the label in the dark, he shook out the main course can and reached behind his neck for the P-38 attached to the back of his compass lanyard. He opened the can, found the plastic spoon, and settled down to a late supper of cold beans and franks.

Fetterman was pleased he'd gotten beans and franks. He'd drawn his rations at random, planning on two meals a day for five days. He knew that there was an excellent chance that lurking somewhere in the depths of his pack was the dreaded ham and lima beans. One meal in every case of twelve was ham and lima beans, and they were indescribably awful, so bad in fact, that the men called them ham and motherfuckers, and frequently had fights over who had to eat them. In three wars, Fetterman had never developed a taste for them. They were like eating gristle mixed with greasy cardboard. They were almost palatable when you could cook them, provided you added enough hot peppers, but not quite. Cold, they were a GI's gastronomic nightmare.

When he'd finished his beans and franks, Fetterman washed them down with a small sip of water from his canteen, then he made sure Schmidt, Smith, and two of the Tais were posted as guard, wrapped himself in his poncho, and tried to sleep.

Fetterman woke with a sudden start to find Schmidt staring him in the face, and was glad he didn't believe in nonsense about vampires. Not even vampires who only imagined they were vampires.

"What is it?" he asked.

"Boats should be here pretty soon. They passed Cao Lanh about twenty minutes ago."

"Twenty minutes? What time is it?"

"It's after four. Something must have held them up. Sergeant Smith said to let you sleep."

"Thanks." Fetterman sat up, checked his weapon to make sure that it was loaded, then rubbed the sleep from his eyes. "Okay. Find Smith and tell him to get his Firefly strobe ready. You got the backup, right?"

"I gave it to Sergeant McMillan. I don't like bright lights."

Fetterman decided he'd better have a talk with Schmidt about this vampire nonsense, but this was not the time to do it.

Fetterman dug his own strobe marker out of the first-aid dressing case on his pistol belt, wrapped his poncho around it, and switched it on. The pulse of light was blinding. Satisfied, he switched it back off.

When Smith arrived, Fetterman made sure all the team members were awake. Then he and Smith, each accompanied by a Tai striker, moved into position at the extreme edges of the river front. As an afterthought, Fetterman had placed McMillan in the center of the dock with the third marker strobe, while the other two Tais and Schmidt covered them with the M-60. Fetterman didn't really feel the precaution was necessary, but there was no sense in taking chances. He also figured having McMillan in the middle of the dock would make matters easier for the boats trying to guide in.

When the boats were still several miles downstream, Schmidt contacted them on the PRC-10, advising them of the change in the marker-light pattern. After a time, they could hear their engines in the distance, and then finally as the boats drew near, the three Special Forces soldiers switched on their tiny strobe-marker lights, each smaller than a cigarette pack, yet producing 200,000 peak lumens, and the Support Flotilla, Special Field Studies Force made port in the thriving necropolis of Ahn Tap.

"H-O-L-Y cats! What hit this place?" said Hooper. "It looks like the dark side of the moon."

He was standing behind the splinter shield of PTGB-73, a mug of steaming black coffee in his hand.

"The gates of hell would be a little more like it," said Fetterman, noting the thick red dust that now covered the blackened timbers and crumbling bamboo walls of Ahn Tap. "There used to be a town of about fifteen hundred people here. A nice little ville for what you get in this part of Vietnam. The VC came in here about a month back with flamethrowers and burned the place to the ground. They didn't let anybody out first, either."

"Nobody?"

"Nobody. We found one little boy hiding under the boat dock. That was all. We found what was left of the rest of the villagers in the old marketplace, about a klick that way."

"Jesus! Why?"

"You mean why did Charlie level this place? Because there's a war on, Lieutenant, and these people picked the wrong side."

"Yah, but I mean, the whole town? It just doesn't make sense."

"It did to the Cong, Lieutenant. They take making war very seriously. The people here got fed up when a few of the local VC executed the schoolteacher and one of the shopkeepers. Some old guy who was apparently highly thought of in the community. They had the audacity to suggest that the Saigon government might be better than the NLF. After that, the villagers denounced the local VC sampan convoys. Charlie didn't like his children acting that way, so he came in and spanked 'em."

Hooper shuddered. "I worked coastal patrol before this. Stopping junks, that kind of thing. I never saw anything like this before. I guess I just never realized how bad it really could be out here in the jungle."

"This isn't really jungle," said Fetterman. "For that you got to go about another dozen miles upstream, toward our camp and the border. This is more like farmland. Sort of the mid-west of the Mekong."

"No thanks. This is close enough for me. You want some coffee, uh, Sergeant, isn't it?"

"Master Sergeant Fetterman. I'm Captain Gerber's team sergeant. Sort of like a CPO. And no thanks, I've had Navy coffee before. It's worse than Army coffee, if that's possible."

It was a little after dawn, and Hooper had just come up on deck when Fetterman strolled by. The Special Forces man hadn't been wearing any rank, but Hooper had made a guess, and been mostly right.

"I thought Gerber was a major."

"It's a temporary rank, like a brevet. When they do promote him, I'll probably have to retire from the Army. Wouldn't want to work for anybody else."

"Is he really that good?"

"Lieutenant," said Fetterman, "I've been in this man's Army for nigh onto twenty-five years, and Mack Gerber beats any goddamned soldier I ever saw. The men'll do anything for him."

"An endorsement like that's hard to argue with. Major Gerber here?"

"No, but I expect he'll be along shortly. I'm sure he'll want to have a final word with your Lieutenant Commander Russell before this show kicks off."

Hooper nodded. "You sure you don't want some coffee? Maybe come aboard and listen to some Stones? I got some great Stones albums."

"Thanks no. My taste runs more to Mozart, Schubert, and Bach. I wouldn't mind having a look at your boat, though."

"Well, then, permission to come aboard granted. Watch yourself on the gangplank."

Hooper gave Fetterman a quick tour of the boat, starting on the foredeck and finishing in the engine room.

"They used to run these things on three twelve-cylinder Packard engines. We use marine diesels now. Not as fast as the old boats I guess, but a lot more efficient."

"I wish Boom-Boom could see this," said Fetterman. "He'd be fascinated by the armament."

"Boom-Boom?"

"Sergeant First Class Tyme, our light weapons expert. Come to think of it, Sergeant Kittredge would probably go ape over those forty mm guns of yours. He's our heavy weapons man."

"We do pack a pretty good punch. Two forties, four twenties, nine fifty cals, and the direct fire eighty-one," Hooper said proudly.

"Yah. Too bad we didn't have this tub when we went up against that river junk."

"How's that?"

"Never mind," said Fetterman. "Just thinking out loud." He changed the subject quickly. "Say, you guys don't have any plasma on board, do you?"

"Plasma? I don't know. Probably. I'd have to check with the corpsman. Why, you guys got wounded?"

"No, but one of our guys is sick. Doc McMillan says he could use a couple units of plasma, and we're about out."

"Well, the aid ship is down at the end. If he's that sick, maybe you should take him there."

"No, no. Nothing like that. He's just a bit weak, really. Has sort of a rare blood disease," Fetterman lied. "It only bothers him once in a while." *Like when the sun is shining*, Fetterman thought.

"Well, I don't know." Hooper looked dubious. "I suppose I could check with the corpsman."

"I sure would appreciate that, Lieutenant. It'd save me a long walk, all the way down to that aid boat you were talking about, and back."

"Okay, I'll have a look. Wait right here." He disappeared below deck, and returned in a few minutes with two plastic Travenol bags. "You said two units of plasma, right?"

"Right, Lieutenant," said Fetterman, taking the IV sets. "Gee thanks. I really do appreciate this." He skipped quickly down the gangplank and started back for the village.

"Hey, wait a minute," Hooper called after him. "The corpsman said he wanted to know what kind of disease your man has. Said he'd never heard of anything like it, and was interested."

"Oh, it's no big thing, Lieutenant," Fetterman called back over his shoulder. "He thinks he's a vampire, that's all." Fetterman put it into high gear, whistling as he double-timed back into the ville.

In mid-afternoon, the first of the strikers began to arrive by helicopter. The choppers came in in flights of ten, with eight to ten Tais in each aircraft. Lieutenant Bao brought the First Independent Tai Strike Company in the initial lift, and Gerber rode in with them for a final word with Russell.

"Just wanted to check with you personally and make sure there were no last minute problems," said Gerber. "My XO, Lieutenant Bromhead, will be in with the next lift. He'll be running one of the strike companies and acting as ground-unit commander for the southern two companies we put in.

Lieutenant Minh, my counterpart, will be bringing in the other company of strikers and the Rangers a little bit later. They'll have the northern prong of the pincers. I'll be in the airborne C and C once we move out."

"Who's in command of the blocking force?"

"That's Lieutenant Hung's Third Independent Tai Strike Company. He'll have Sergeants Anderson and Kittredge and a mortar platoon with him. We're also going to send Sergeant Xuyen along, he's communications, and Sergeant Tam, medical specialist. They'll be inserted by helicopter according to the prearranged schedule. All your people got their SOIs?"

"Affirmative."

"Well, that's it then. Good luck, Commander."

"Good luck to you too, Major. I hope you find what you're looking for."

"I hope we find something."

At 0400 hours, the men were loaded aboard the ATCs, which had been refueled during the morning and afternoon from the LCM tanker, and at 0430 the flotilla sailed, preceded by Hooper's gunboats and Gomoll's section of SWIFT boats, with the other two SWIFT-boat sections serving as flank security.

The floating howitzer battery was detached at the mouth of the canal, and at exactly 0630 the artillery bombardment began.

The first indication that Major Huynh Dong Long, commander of the 129th Viet Cong Main Force Battalion, had that today was not going to be a good day was when he was awakened from a sound sleep by an ARVN 105mm howitzer shell blowing in the roof of his command bunker.

CHAPTER 19

THE KINH KY CANAL, NORTH OF CHO MOI

As the ramp of the armored troop carrier dropped into the shallow water of the canal, Bromhead, bayonet fixed to his M-14 rifle, yelled "Follow me!" and charging down the ramp, sloshed through the dirty muck and onto the greasy bank.

Behind him, Fetterman glanced at Tyme. "Well, that's the way John Wayne woulda done it."

Tyme racked back the slide on his shotgun, chambering a shell, and jammed another round of #4 buckshot into the magazine. "*Di di!*" he called over his shoulder to the strikers. "*Mau len!*"

The Special Forces men splashed ashore, and the Tai soldiers followed.

On both sides of them, 400 men, shouting, yelling, and screaming like banshees clambered up the slippery dike and swarmed onto the marshy plain beyond. They made less than fifty yards before coming under intense crossfire from automatic weapons bunkers, well concealed amid the tall grass, and firing almost at ground level.

Schmidt, looking as anemic as a leukemia victim as he humped the radio at Bromhead's elbow, gave the lieutenant a surprisingly strong push to the ground and loosed a long burst of return fire from his M-60, temporarily suppressing the enemy gunners and allowing the other men to drop to the ground before seeking cover himself.

All the men were down and firing now; they didn't have any clear targets, but were putting rounds out into the high grass in front of them.

"Vo! Let those bastards know we don't appreciate their welcome!" Bromhead yelled to the LLDB Sergeant who was carrying an M-79.

Vo nodded, grabbed two strikers who were also carrying M-79s, and all three men began firing grenades into the brush, starting almost at the minimum safe distance of thirty-one meters and slowly working their way out to 150.

Schmidt abruptly stuck out the radio handset to Bromhead, said "Gunboats," and jammed a long belt of ammo into the M-60.

"Barracuda, this is Land Crab. We're taking fire from bunkers to our left front and far right flank. All the way from danger close on out to the treeline. How about putting some discouragement in there for us," said Bromhead.

"That's a rog., Land Crab. Hang tight. Mother's little helper is on the way."

The PTGBs and SWIFT boats made a pass down the canal behind the ATCs, firing mortars, machine guns, and automatic cannon. The 40mm tracers floated out majestically, like big red softballs, while the 20mm stuff seemed more like somebody spitting Ping-Pong balls, and the 50s looked like a swarm of angry red bees. The cannon and mortar shells chewed up ground, blew up soggy chunks of marsh grass and geysers of water, and chopped down trees and bamboo. They did everything except silence the enemy machine guns.

At the end of their run, the boats turned sharply in the narrow canal and came back for another pass.

While the boats were pounding the high grass, searching by fire for the bunkers concealed there, Bromhead reported to

Gerber in the C and C helicopter overhead that they had heavy contact with the enemy.

Gerber was aware that the southern arm of his planned pincer movement had been stalled almost on the beachhead. To the north, Minh was having better luck. His troops were able to advance several hundred yards inland before contacting the enemy. Lieutenant Hung's blocking force was in position, but as yet had no contact and had not found any suitable targets for their mortar platoon.

Although Gerber could not locate the bunkers firing in the high grass from the air, he was able to see the enemy troop movement along the edge of the woods on Bromhead's southern flank, and directed open-sheaf artillery fire from the 105s into the treeline.

The ATCs, which had covered the initial phase of the beach assault with their .50-cal. machine guns, started taking mortar fire from VC positions firing through clearings deep in the woods, and had to be withdrawn to the river. They were sitting ducks if left beached against the canal bank.

The technicians aboard the C and C boat with Russell were able to get a plot on the mortar positions with the new counter mortar radar. Since the 105s and gunboats were otherwise engaged, UH-1B helicopter gunships, each equipped with four M-60 machine guns and 2.75-inch rockets, were called in to suppress the VC mortars, which they successfully did.

As the ATCs backed away from the canal bank, the gunboats made another run to cover their withdrawal and provide continued suppression on the bunkers in the high grass to Bromhead's front. As they did so, they came under recoilless rifle fire from two positions concealed on the opposite bank of the canal. One SWIFT boat was hit and blown almost in half, its crew flung into the water.

Hooper veered his boat sharply, and brought it into the reedy area along the bank of the canal, right under one of the recoilless rifles, the forward 40mm and 20mm mounts firing into the position at point-blank range, destroying it utterly.

The second VC recoilless crew was alert, however, and scored a direct hit on the wheelhouse of PTGB-73. Hooper was decapitated by the blast, and his coxswain mortally wounded by a deadly shower of steel splinters.

Jack Gomolls's SWIFT boat, accompanied by Spike Patterson's section and the other PTGB roared down on the recoilless position like revenge-minded sharks, hammering the bunker with an incredible concentration of firepower until nothing remained but finely powdered dirt.

"Boom-Boom, I don't know about you, but I think I've about had enough of this shit," said Fetterman. "What say you and I work our way around to the left and see if we can get behind those guys in that bunker?"

Tyme nodded his agreement, and accompanied by a squad of Tais, they began to work their way in on the machine gun that had pinned down most of their platoon.

They low-crawled through the wet grass, hearing the whine of bullets whipping past them less than a foot overhead and cursing the buttons on their fatigues for holding them up so high. When they had gone about seventy yards, Fetterman spotted the flickering muzzle of the RPD. The gunner, obviously inexperienced, was hosing down the whole area, rather than firing in short, controlled bursts, and the sustained flare of hot gases from the barrel was giving away his position. He'd been hard to spot so far only because his firing port was so close to the ground.

With the Tais covering, Fetterman and Tyme worked their way close enough to lob a couple of smoke grenades in front of the bunker. When they popped and billowed, obscuring the gunner's vision with dense clouds of green smoke, Fetterman dashed forward and rolled a fragmentation grenade inside the gun port. As soon as it detonated, Tyme located the camouflage matting concealing the bunker entrance, threw it aside, and dropped into the bunker, shotgun ready.

Fetterman heard the boom-boom, boom-boom, boom-boom of Tyme's Remington thundering in the enclosed space of the bunker, and followed, submachine gun ready to fire instantly. He dropped into a surprisingly large bunker, filled with smoke and dust, in time to see Tyme toss a grenade through what appeared to be a hole in the wall.

"Outside!" Tyme yelled, and the two men scrambled topside as the grenade exploded. "Interconnecting tunnel," Tyme explained. "The whole area is probably honeycombed with them."

To the north, near the river, Lieutenant Minh was having his own problems. After an initially rapid advance, he'd run into stiff resistance from an extensive bunker complex, just as he'd started the swing-in of his leg of the pincer movement.

Gerber saw that he was stymied, and immediately radioed Russell.

"Pelican Six, this is Blackhawk. Put the reserves in at grid reference two-four-six-one-three-five. Tell them I'll meet them there."

"Roger Blackhawk. Understand two-four-six-one-three-five."

Gerber leaned forward and tapped the AC on the shoulder. "Can you put us down in that little open area just to the right of the small cut down there?"

"I can't land it," the warrant officer shouted back over the roar of the turbine. "There's nothing solid to put it on. Get you down to a couple of feet though, and you can jump off the skid. You sure you want to go down there?"

Gerber nodded. "Not want to, have to. Pull back and orbit over the river after you let us out. We may want you to come pick us up again."

"Roger that."

Gerber turned to Bocker. "Galvin, warm up that backpack of yours, I think we're going to need it."

Bocker nodded and switched on the PRC-10.

The helicopter dropped them off just as Sergeant Krung led the two platoons of strikers ashore from the reserve ATCs. Krung hadn't been happy about being assigned to command the reaction force, fearing it would keep him out of the battle. Now he positively beamed at the prospect of finally getting the chance to kill some more communists.

Gerber, having anticipated the possibility of bunkers, had heavily armed the reserve force with equipment that included four 3.5-inch rocket launchers and four M2A1-7 flamethrowers. They advanced rapidly across the marshy area on Minh's left flank, and hit the bunkers from the side.

The roof was blown completely off the first bunker by one of the Tai bazooka teams, and a squad of strikers, led by Krung, rushed forward, riddling the VC who had been inside with automatic fire from their M-2 carbines. Quickly they fell into a pattern of hitting a bunker with one of the bazookas, then rushing in to kill the survivors. Other teams squirted streams of liquid fire through the open gun ports of the bunkers, incinerating the Viet Cong inside.

The smell of cordite and the stench of burning flesh filled the air, mingling with the sharp aroma of napalm. And through the gunpowder haze, the dust and smoke of it all, Gerber could see a grimly satisfied Sergeant Krung, pausing occasionally to claim trophies from those he had personally killed.

The fighting raged throughout the morning, but tapered off abruptly in early afternoon when about a company of surviving Viet Cong decided that it was time to run away. They ran smack into Lieutenant Hung's blocking force, and the intense fire from the 81mm mortars, superbly directed by Kittredge, chopped them up into very tiny pieces before they even got within small arms range. After that, the remainder of the battle consisted mostly of the laborious process of clearing tunnels of stragglers, and inventorying the stockpile of VC supplies before demolition.

Fetterman couldn't believe the extent of the supply cache and bunker complex. There were literally dozens of tons of ammunition, foodstuffs, and arms. There were cases of SKS carbines and AK-47s still packed in the Chinese equivalent of Cosmoline, crates of hand grenades, and cases of medical supplies, many of them bearing United States markings. In one underground bunker, they found a small field hospital, complete with a two-table operating room. The most interesting find, however, was several wooden boxes containing supplies of piastres and MPC. Fetterman didn't know if they were real or counterfeit, but estimated there was nearly a hundred thousand dollars' worth.

Late in the afternoon, they came upon the ruined command bunker, and found a body in it that Sergeant Tran positively identified as being that of Major Huynh Dong Long, commander of the VC 129th Main Force Battalion. From the wreckage atop the body, it was obvious that he had been killed sometime during the first few minutes of battle when an artillery round had struck the bunker and collapsed the roof, leaving Gerber to wonder who had directed the determined defense of the complex.

Fetterman had no such doubts. In a bunker containing a small underground mess hall, he had discovered a large bowl of rice, peppers, and fish, with a now cold, but full, cup of tea beside it. Lying next to the teacup had been a khaki uniform cap. It was the style worn by Chinese officers.

CHAPTER 20

SPECIAL FORCES CAMP A-555

The mission was over. The raid had been a spectacular success. They had captured or destroyed thirty-seven tons of supplies, and eliminated the VC 129th Main Force Battalion as an effective fighting unit. In the process, they had proven the validity of the mobile riverine force concept; there were still many problems to be solved, but the groundwork had all been laid, and the idea was combat tested. Gerber should have been feeling very pleased.

He wasn't.

Right now there was a combination early Christmas party and victory celebration going on over in the team bunker. Lieutenant Colonel Bates had flown in a bunch of canned hams and beer, and the men were in a pretty upbeat mood that had been heightened by word of Minh's promotion to captain, and confirmation that he would remain at Camp A-555 as Vietnamese commander.

The victory had not been without cost, however. Casualties among the strikers had been moderate, a catchword the Saigon command preferred to use when they meant fairly heavy. Clearing the bunker complexes and tunnels had proven to be a risky proposition, due chiefly to booby traps left behind by the Viet Cong when they abandoned their base.

One such device had claimed Schmidt, the new communications specialist who had affected such weird dress and habits, but had such outstanding eyes. It hadn't even been a sophisticated device. Just a giant crossbow attached to a tripwire he'd stumbled over. It had driven a four-foot-long wooden bolt through his chest.

The men had been troubled by his death — as much by the nature of it as by the fact that he was one of their own. But Schmidt was still just an FNG, and the wake hadn't lasted long. They would remember him because he was so unusual, but they had grieved for him, and drank the Beam's to him, as was his due, and it was time to get on with business.

The battle had also cost the life of Lieutenant Rhee, commander of the ARVN Ranger company who had fought with distinction under Minh's direction. He had been killed rushing a machine gun bunker.

There were a host of others.

Anderson was wounded. It wasn't serious, but it had cut an ugly gouge along his left forearm. He seemed inordinately pleased with it. It meant he was no longer cherry, he said. The men couldn't call him a new guy anymore.

Tyme had been quick to point out that while that was true, they could call him something else, and a contest had been organized to pick a nickname for the newest member of Gerber's A-team. As yet, there was no winner, for which Anderson was grateful.

Practically the only people who weren't raising a great deal of hoopla, were Fetterman and Gerber.

Fetterman was spending a quiet moment with Le Quan Kim, the young Vietnamese boy he had decided to adopt, after presenting him with his Christmas gift, a Swiss army knife that Fetterman himself had carried for years. He had considered giving the boy a puppy to replace the one that had been killed, he could have gotten one from one of the strikers' families, but common sense had prevailed. There was still the possibility that Le would have to spend some time in the Can Tho orphanage before the necessary paperwork could be completed, and in that instance, a dog would be out of the question. Besides, if the adoption was approved, Le would be going to the States soon, and wouldn't be able to take an animal with him. There would be plenty of time for pets later.

The boy surprised Fetterman with a gift of his own, a handmade crossbow that he had obviously spent a great many hours manufacturing. Like the Swiss army knife, it was a gift given with practicality in mind. The boy knew Fetterman's profession well enough to know what the crossbow would likely be used for. His understanding of the sentiment of the gift had moved the master sergeant almost to tears.

Gerber wasn't partying either. He simply wasn't in a partying mood. He'd known briefly the exhilaration of a job well done, of victory achieved over the enemy in battle, the laudatory comments of Colonel Bates and General Hull, and unbelievably, even Crinshaw, who had condescended to send the one word message, "Congratulations."

He'd drunk the toast to the departed with the men, had a couple of beers, and extended his own heartfelt congratulations to Minh, both on the operation and on the Vietnamese lieutenant's promotion to captain. Then he'd slipped off quietly to be with his own thoughts.

He knew he should be happy. Intellectually, he knew that. He was everybody's man-of-the-hour.

Everybody's but one.

Karen Morrow was alive. She and three other survivors of the plane crash had been found by a patrol led by Dave Henderson's executive officer, Lieutenant Bunnell. Before being rescued, they'd spent five days in the jungle without food and very little water, hiding from Viet Cong patrols looking for them.

Gerber had felt a great sense of elation when he learned the news. Henderson had called him on the HORN and given him the word as soon as Bunnell had brought them into the camp at Dak To. Then he'd asked if Gerber wanted to talk with her.

He had.

She hadn't.

It had hurt, and he hadn't gotten over it yet.

Christ, how it hurt! He didn't know how to deal with unrequited love.

Dead bodies were his stock in trade. Dead VC, dead ARVN, dead Tais, dead Americans. Dead, dead, dead.

A body was something you could understand, something you could put your foot on and count. Something that had no mysteries left. Something that couldn't hurt you, or feel hurt itself.

Gerber was tired.

He was tired of having to fight Crinshaw for every little scrap of supplies he needed to keep his camp running.

He was tired of having to fight the Army for the right to fight the war in a winnable manner when he knew it could be won but was prevented from doing so by senseless regulations and the opinions of the press.

He was tired of seeing good men die. First Schattschneider, then Clarke, and now Schmidt. And young Sean Cavanaugh, who might as well be dead; he was a near vegetable in the psychiatric ward of Saigon Military Hospital. He'd lost Wilson and Forbes, who he'd been responsible for, even if they weren't his men, and the young helicopter pilot whose name escaped him. Was it Ramsey or Chrisman? And all the others besides. The loss of each of them cut him like a knife.

Perhaps somebody with his kind of feelings didn't belong in his line of work.

It was too late in the game to worry about that kind of thing now. It was too late to do anything.

Except perhaps stop the hurt.

In the only way he knew how.

Gerber picked up the bottle of Beam's Choice from his desk drawer, and eyed it speculatively. There were about three inches of liquor remaining in the bottom. He uncapped it, and drank it down in a single gulp. Then he wiped his lip with the tips of his fingers.

"Smooth," he whispered to himself.

Then he picked up the Colt .45 pistol from the desktop, jacked a round into the chamber, and stepped out into the star-studded Southeast Asian night.

GLOSSARY

AC — Aircraft commander. The pilot in charge of the aircraft.
AFVN — The Armed Forces radio and television network in Vietnam. Army PFC Pat Sajak was probably the most memorable of the AFVN DJs with his loud and long, "GOOOOOOOOOOD MORNING Vietnam!" The spinning Wheel of Fortune leaves no clue about his whereabouts today.
A-GUNNER — Assistant gunner. Assists the man who operates the machine gun.
AK-47 — Assault rifle normally used by the North Vietnamese and the Viet Cong.
AO — Area of operations.
AO DAI — A long, dress-like garment, split up the sides and worn over pants.
AP ROUNDS — Armor piercing ammunition.
AR-15 — An early model of the M-16.
ARVN — Army of the Republic of Vietnam. A South Vietnamese soldier. Also known as Marvin Arvin.
ASAP — As soon as possible.
ATC — Armored troop carrier. A lightly armored and armed landing craft used to transport troops in riverine operations.
BAC SI — Vietnamese for doctor.
BAR — Browning Automatic Rifle.
BAZOOKA — Common name for the 2.75-inch and 3.5-inch rocket launchers developed during World War II for use against tanks. Also used against other vehicles, fortifications, and boats, and when firing WP rounds against personnel.
BEAUCOUP — Many.

BODY COUNT — The number of enemy killed, wounded or captured during an operation. Used by Saigon and Washington as a means of measuring progress of the war.

BOOM-BOOM — Term used by the Vietnamese prostitutes in selling their product.

BOQ — Bachelor Officers' Quarters.

C and C — The command and control aircraft that circles overhead to direct the combined air and ground operations.

CARIBOU — Cargo transport plane.

CHINOOK — Army Aviation twin engine helicopter. A CH-47.

CLAYMORE — An antipersonnel mine that fires 750 steel balls with a lethal range of fifty meters.

COMMO — Short for communications.

DAI UY — Vietnamese Army rank the equivalent of captain.

DEROS — Date of estimated return from overseas. It was the date a person would return from Vietnam.

FCT — Fire control tower.

FIVE — Radio call sign for the executive officer of a unit.

FIVE O'CLOCK FOLLIES — A derogatory term that referred to the press conferences held in Vietnam.

FNG — A fucking new guy.

FOB — Forward operating base.

FOUR CORPS — The Mekong River Delta region of Vietnam.

FRENCH FORT — A distinctive, triangular-shaped structure built by the hundreds by the French.

GARAND — The M-1 rifle that was replaced by the M-14. Issued to the Vietnamese early in the war.

GUNBOAT — Any small heavily armed vessel. Especially one for use in riverine operations.

GUNSHIP — A helicopter, such as the UH-1B, or cargo aircraft such as the AC-47 converted for the air support role by the addition of machine guns, miniguns, or rockets.

HE — High-explosive ammunition.

HOOTCH — Almost any shelter, from temporary to long term.

HORN — A radio communications network used in Vietnam.

HOTEL THREE — A helicopter landing area at Saigon's Tan Son Nhut airport.

HUEY — A UH-1 helicopter.

INCOUNTRY — Term used to refer to American troops operating in South Vietnam. They were all incountry.

INTELLIGENCE — Any information about the enemy operations. It can include troop movements, weapons capabilities, biographies of enemy commanders, and general information about terrain features. It is any information that would be useful in planning a mission.

K-BAR — A type of military combat knife.

KIMCHI — Korean delicacy smelling like nuoc mam. To be "in deep kimchi" was to be in serious trouble.

KIA — Killed in action.

KLICK — A thousand meters. A kilometer.

LAMBRETTA — Small, open vehicle used for transportation. A glorified three-wheeled scooter.

LIMA — Land line. Refers to telephone communications between two points on ground.

LBJ — Long Binh Jail.

LCM — Landing craft medium, men, or mechanized.

LEGS — Derogatory term used by airborne qualified troops in talking about regular infantry.

LLDB — Luc Luong Dac Biet. The South Vietnamese Special Forces.

LP — Listening Post. A position outside the perimeter manned by a couple of people to give advance warning of enemy activity.

LZ — Landing zone.

M-3 — .45-caliber submachine gun, sometimes called a grease gun.

M-14 — Standard rifle of the U.S., eventually replaced by the M-16. It fired the standard NATO round: 7.62mm.

M-16 — Became the standard infantry weapon of the Vietnam War. It fired the 5.56mm ammunition.

M-60 — A light, general-purpose machine gun firing the same ammunition as the M-14 rifle. It became the standard squad automatic weapon of U.S. and South Vietnamese troops during the Vietnam war, replacing the BAR and .30-cal. Browning light machine gun.

M-79 — A short barrel, shoulder-fired weapon that fires a 40mm grenade. These can be high explosives, white phosphorus, or canister.

MACV — Military Assistance Command, Vietnam, replaced MAAG in 1964.

MEDCAP — Medical Civic Action Program.

MEDEVAC — Medical Evacuation. Also called Dust-Off. A helicopter used to take the wounded to the medical facilities.

MG — Machine gun.

MPC — Military Payment Certificate — paper money, sometimes called monopoly money — issued in lieu of regular currency.

NAG — Naval Advisory Group. U.S. personnel who advised the South Vietnamese military on matters maritime.

NCO — A noncommission officer. A noncom. A sergeant.

NEXT — The man who said he was the next to be rotated home. *See* Short.

NINETEEN — The average age of the combat soldier in Vietnam, as opposed to twenty-six in World War II.

NLF — National Liberation Front.

NUOC MAM — A fish sauce used by the Vietnamese.

NVA — The North Vietnamese Army. Also used to designate a soldier from North Vietnam.

OPEN SHEAF — Term used for artillery fire spread out along an axis, rather than concentrated on a point target.

P-38 — Military designation for the small, two-piece cart opener supplied with C-rations.

PCOD — Personnel coming off duty.

PIASTRE — South Vietnamese monetary unit worth slightly less than one cent.

PITA — Problem people. From pain-in-the lower posterior region.

POGUES — A derogatory term used to describe the fat, lazy people who inhabited rear areas, taking all the best supplies for themselves, and leaving the rest for the men in the field.

PRC-10 — Man-portable radio.

PTGB — Patrol Torpedo Gunboat. A World War II vintage torpedo boat about eighty feet long, converted to the gunboat role by the removal of torpedoes and depth charges, and mounting .50-cal. machine guns, 20mm and 40mm cannon, and sometimes rocket launchers or 81mm direct fire mortars. The forerunner of the Monitor riverboats used in Vietnam after 1966.

PUNGI STAKE — Sharpened bamboo hidden to penetrate the foot, sometimes dipped in feces.

R and R — Rest and relaxation. The term came to mean a trip outside of Vietnam where the soldier could forget about the war.

RF STRIKERS — Local military forces recruited and employed inside a province. Known as Regional Forces.

RIVER RAIDER I — First official joint Army-Navy riverine operation conducted in the upper Long Tau shipping channel and in the Southwestern Run Sat Special Zone, Feb. 16–Mar. 20, 1967, which led to the formation of the Mobile Riverine Force.

RPD — Soviet light machine gun, 7.62mm.

RPG — Rocket-propelled grenade, or its launcher. Bazooka-like weapon used by the VC and NVA.

RTO — Radio telephone operator. The radioman of a unit.

RULES OF ENGAGEMENT — The rules that told the American troops when they could fire and when they couldn't. Full Suppression meant they could fire all the way in on a landing. Normal Rules meant they could return fire for fire received. Negative Suppression meant they weren't to shoot back.

SAPPER — An enemy soldier used in demolitions. Uses explosives during attacks.

SFOB — Special Forces Operating Base.

SHORT — Term used by everyone in Vietnam to tell all who would listen that his tour was about over.

SHORT-TIMER — Person who has been in Vietnam for nearly a year and who would be rotated back to the World soon.

SIX — Radio call signed for the unit commander.

SKS — Soviet-made carbine.

SLICK — Helicopter used to carry troops or supplies. Not a gunship or medevac.

SMG — Submachine gun.

SOI — Signal Operating Instructions. The booklet that contained the call signs and radio frequencies of the units in Vietnam.

SONG TIEN GIANG — Vietnamese for "The north river." The Mekong. Song Hau Giang or the south river, is Vietnamese for the Bassac.

STAND TO — Practice of having personnel man their weapons positions from one half hour before dawn or dusk until one half hour after, to prevent personnel moving about a camp and thus providing easy targets for enemy snipers to shoot at and then slip away.

STEEL POT — The standard U.S. Army helmet. The steel pot was the outer, metal cover.

SWEDISH K — An SMG similar to the M-3, except 9mm. Often fitted with a noise suppressor or silencer.

SWIFT BOAT — Small, fast boat powered by twin diesel engines used for coastal patrol and riverine operations in Vietnam. They carried a seven-man crew, and were usually armed with two .50-cal. machine guns, M-60 machine guns, and an 81mm direct fire mortar. Later versions also carried an automatic 40mm grenade launcher.

TAI — A Vietnamese ethnic group living in the mountainous regions.

TDY — A temporary duty assignment away from one's normal duty station. A TDY could be for any length of time less than a year. Ninety days was typical.

THREE — Radio call sign of the Operations Officer.

THREE CORPS — The military area around Saigon. Vietnam was divided into four corps areas.

THE WORLD — The United States.

TOC — Tactical operations center.

TO&E — Table of Organization and Equipment.

TRUNG UY — Vietnamese Army rank equal to a lieutenant.

TWO — Radio call sign of the Intelligence officer.

UH-1B — A Bravo model of the HUEY helicopter.

VC — Viet Cong, called Victor Charlie (phonetic alphabet), or just Charlie.

VIET CONG — A contraction of Vietnam Cong San (Vietnamese Communist).

VIET CONG SAN — The Vietnamese communists. A term in use since 1956.

VIETMINH — Name used by the Vietnamese communists fighting the French in the early 1950s and by which the VC and NVA were still known in Laos during the Vietnam war.

VNAF — South Vietnamese Air Force.

VOQ — Visiting Officers' Quarters.

WILLY PETE — WP, White phosphorus, called smoke rounds. Also used as antipersonnel weapons.

XO — The executive officer of a unit. The Five, or second in command.

A NOTE TO THE READER

Dear Reader,

If you have enjoyed this novel enough to leave a review on **Amazon** and **Goodreads**, then we would be truly grateful.

Sapere Books

SAPERE
BOOKS